The last remnants of sanity were fleeing fast...

For the first time in her life Tracy knew the need for fulfillment. *I'm shameless*, she thought, *and I don't care.* Their lovemaking had never been more erotic, or more tender.

Once she'd resisted him, not wanting to be one in a procession of females. Now even that thought no longer seemed to matter.

Ryan pulled away from her with a sudden shuddering groan. "I want you to marry me," he said. "Soon!" he insisted.

She smiled suddenly, radiantly. But there was also confusion. "Ryan... why?"

"Isn't it obvious?" he demanded huskily. "I want you in my bed."

To Tracy there was only one obvious reason for marriage, and that was love. But never once had Ryan given her any indication that her feelings were reciprocated....

Books by Rosemary Carter

HARLEQUIN PRESENTS

HARLEQUIN ROMANCE

These books may be available at your local bookseller.

Don't miss any of our special offers. Write to us at the following address for information on our newest releases.

Harlequin Reader Service
P.O. Box 52040, Phoenix, AZ 85072-2040
Canadian address: P.O. Box 2800, Postal Station A,
5170 Yonge St., Willowdale, Ont. M2N 6J3

ROSEMARY CARTER

impetuous marriage

Harlequin Books

TORONTO • NEW YORK • LONDON
AMSTERDAM • PARIS • SYDNEY • HAMBURG
STOCKHOLM • ATHENS • TOKYO • MILAN

Harlequin Presents first edition November 1985
ISBN 0-373-10831-1

Original hardcover edition published in 1985
by Mills & Boon Limited

CHAPTER ONE

'ALLISON'S eloped.'

Tracy Galland gripped the telephone tightly with one hand while with the other she pushed a thick swathe of honey-coloured hair from her puckered forehead.

'I don't believe you're serious.'

'It's true, I tell you. Tracy, you have to stop them.'

Her mother *was* serious, Tracy decided, catching the sincerity in the panic-stricken tone. What had her young sister been up to this time?

'You have to go after them!' Lucille Galland said again.

'It's hard to discuss this on the phone.' Tracy glanced at Dean, who was watching her with a mixture of amusement and impatience.

'You'll leave today?'

'I'm working, Mom.'

'That nice young man will understand.'

Impatience was rapidly becoming the dominant expression in Dean's face. Studio time was expensive, and a struggling young photographer had to think of costs.

'I'll be at the house by four.' Tracy flexed a shapely leg that had become stiff from remaining too long in one pose. 'Mom—please try to relax. Getting yourself worked up will achieve nothing.'

'Trouble?' Dean asked, as she came back to him, and tried to recapture her position on the white hammock.

'My sister has run off. Eloped, Mom says.'

'Light's fading,' was the only response. 'You had

5

the left leg bent not the right one.' Tracy changed positions and the camera clicked. 'Ah, that's good, honey. Smile. Lovely. One more.'

The camera clicked, one, two, three, in quick succession, while Tracy kept both the pose and the smile. 'Marvellous. That leg again. Ah, right. Sensational.'

And then the session was over, and Tracy relaxed, the slender tanned body leaving the hammock in a graceful movement that reminded the watching man of a dancer.

'That was great,' Dean said. 'I'll work in the darkroom tonight. Can't wait to see the results.' He came to her. 'Let's have something to eat in the meantime, I'm starving, we both are. You've been marvellous, Tracy, you can name the restaurant.'

She smiled up at him as she slipped on a light corduroy jacket. 'I have to get home, but thanks anyway.'

'You really believe your sister has eloped? You can't be serious.'

'My mother sounded serious. In fact she sounded rather desperate.'

'And now she wants to talk to you about it?'

'More than talk.' Tracy made a rueful face. 'She wants me to stop them.'

'Try stopping two determined people.' Dean was amused.

'I may have to try.'

'You sound as if you mean it.'

'I do.'

The laughter left the young man's eyes as he put his hands on her shoulders. 'You can't just leave here, Tracy.'

'I may have to.' Green eyes, the colour of emeralds, were troubled.

'Just what do you intend doing?'

'I won't know that till I've spoken to my mother.'

'Would you really go after Allison?'

'I don't know.'

'You've work to do here, Tracy.'

She shifted beneath his hands. 'We've wrapped up this photo session, Dean.'

'I'm hoping to get something else lined up.'

'You may have to look for another model, if only for the next assignment.'

'You're my favourite.' The look he gave her was only partly professional. They had been dating for almost three months, and Dean made no secret of the attraction Tracy held for him. 'Why did Allison have to do such a silly thing?' he asked.

Green eyes sparkled suddenly. 'It's not the first silly thing she's done. I adore my young sister, but it seems to me sometimes that I've spent much of my life getting her out of scrapes. This is the first time she's rushed into an impetuous marriage, though.'

Strong hands tightened on her shoulders, drawing her to him. 'I wish I could persuade *you* into an impetuous marriage, Tracy love.'

She laughed softly as she let herself rest against him. 'Two run-away marriages might be more than my mother could stand.'

'Doesn't need to be a run-away affair.' His tone had grown serious. 'I want to marry you, Tracy.'

'Dean . . .' She pulled a little away from him, tensing as she always did when the subject of marriage was mentioned.

'Just say the word, honey.'

'I can't . . .'

'Not with your mother waiting for you,' he agreed. As if he sensed her resistance and impatience, the hands that held her loosened their grip. 'When you've brought Allison safely back home, maybe we can talk again.'

'Dean . . .'

'Think about it, honey, that's all I ask.' He grinned down at her, but his tone was a little ragged. 'Just don't take too long.'

What was stopping her from saying yes to Dean? she wondered, as she emerged from the building and began to make her way to the bus-stop. They had so much in common. Too much she thought sometimes, for when they talked it was as if their thoughts on most things were similar. She could anticipate his comments before he made them, which did not make for stimulating conversation. They both enjoyed music and dancing and swimming, and when he kissed her that was enjoyable too. But not electrifying. Perhaps if it had been more electrifying it would not be so easy to resist his efforts to get her to go to bed with him. But then perhaps enjoyment was the most one could hope for in a relationship. Maybe the passions she'd read about, and which she dimly perceived as being dormant in herself, were not part of real life. Maybe she was silly to hold out on Dean when she knew they could be happy together.

She stopped at a crossing and gave her head a shake, her thick fair hair bouncing on her shoulders as she did so. Why was she thinking about Dean? No decision had to be made today. It was Allison who should be occupying her thoughts, Allison and a man whose name she did not know, and who might conceivably already be Tracy's brother-in-law. The crossing was clear and Tracy crossed the road, walking suddenly faster.

The streets of Durban were crowded with people going home from work, and many were the male glances that rested appreciatively on the tall young girl with hair the colour of liquid honey, and a graceful figure that was rounded in all the right places. Tracy would have been amazed to know how many men thought her beautiful. At twenty-two she knew that she was considered attractive, knew too that there was something piquantly different about her face, which accounted for the fact that she was in demand as a photographic model. But beautiful was not a word that she would have applied to herself. Of the two sisters it was Allison who was beautiful.

Whereas Tracy was tall and graceful, Allison was tiny and delicate and very pretty. Resilient enough when she had to be, she nevertheless had a fragile appearance that made men fall over themselves to protect her. And Allison loved their protectiveness. She had had many boyfriends, but eloping was something new and different, making Tracy wonder about the man who had convinced her sister to take such an extraordinary step.

'His name is Derrick Demant,' said her mother, when Tracy had settled her with tea and a biscuit.

'Demant?' Tracy was thoughtful. 'The name rings no bell. A new boyfriend?'

'Fairly new. Because you're always at your flat you haven't run into him. Allie didn't talk about him often, but I've met him once or twice. What are we going to do?'

'Nothing in a hurry.' Tracy's voice was firm as she made an effort to calm her mother. 'How do you know it's serious?'

'She left a letter.'

'In true dramatic Allison fashion,' Tracy said drily.

'Don't joke at a time like this.' Lucille Galland looked tense.

'I'm sorry.' Tracy felt a pang of remorse as she noted her mother's white face. 'Tell me what happened.'

'As I said, she left a letter. Such a serious-sounding letter. There's also a photo. I'll show them to you.'

Reading the letter, Tracy registered the thread of

seriousness which made her mother believe that Allison meant to go through with the marriage. There was nothing dramatic about it after all. She loved Derrick, she said, and she was going to marry him.

My future brother-in-law? Tracy wondered, as she picked up the photo and wished that she could see Derrick Demant's features more clearly. The photo had been taken by a novice, for it was out of focus and there was light and shade in all the wrong places. Derrick towered above Allison. He was smiling down at her, and his arm was around her shoulders. He was tall, his hair was dark, and he had the slightly awkward look of a young man who had not yet become altogether comfortable with his height and the power of his body.

'Can't tell much from this,' she said, looking across at her mother.

'*I* can tell you something. He's a fortune-hunter.'

Tracy stared at her mother. 'I beg your pardon!'

'He's after Tracy's money.'

'Uncle Ned's legacy?' Tracy burst out laughing, and was sorry a moment later when she saw her mother's hurt face. 'It's hardly a fortune,' she said.

'Not what some might call a fortune, maybe, but everything is relative. To a young farm labourer five thousand more or less is not to be sneezed at.' She pushed a distraught hand through her hair. 'Will you go after them, Tracy?'

Tracy's laughter vanished as she sat forward in her chair. 'They could be married by now.'

'Heaven forbid!'

'You've given me nothing to go on. What do you know about Derrick Demant? Who is he? Where have they gone? The letter doesn't say.'

'He lives at a farm called Umhlowi. Somewhere on the South Coast. The nearest biggest village could be Ifafa Beach.'

'That's his home?'

'It's where he works as far as I could gather.'

'Anything else?'

'He's in his early twenties. Allison's crazy about him, and she seems to think the feeling's mutual.'

'In that case the marriage might not be as disastrous as you think.'

'Tracy!'

'You really think he's a fortune-hunter?'

Her mother hesitated. 'Yes, I do. He's deliberately swept Allie off her feet. There has to be a reason for this head-long rush into madness.'

Useless to point out to her mother in this emotion-charged moment that perhaps it was not head-long after all, that it was possible that Derrick Demant was the right man for Allison. For now the first priority was to find her sister, and to discover whether marriage was what she really wanted, or whether, in a mood of romantic impulsiveness, she had let a momentary whim determine the course of her life.

'Have you thought of the fact that Allie isn't eighteen yet?' she asked. 'She can't get married without your permission.'

'She could lie about her age.'

'I don't believe she'd do that.'

'Tracy, please, you know I can't get away from the boutique. When can you leave?'

Tracy drew a breath that was something between a laugh and a sigh. Did her mother understand what she was asking of her? Did she really think that her daughter could go, at a moment's notice, to a farm that was 'somewhere near Ifafa Beach'?

'I have a flat,' she said.

'I'll water the plants and feed the cat.'

'I also have to speak to Dean.'

'Dean, yes . . .'

'I do have a job,' Tracy reminded patiently.

'Can't it wait?'

'If we were in the midst of something important I might say no. As it is we were just wrapping up a session.'

Lucille smiled her relief. 'It's simple then.'

Nothing was ever quite that simple, Tracy thought later, as she sat in the garden and stared through the darkness. The African sky was ablaze with stars, and the air had lost none of its daytime heat, for this was Natal, the sugar-cane belt of South Africa, where the weather was often muggily hot for months on end without respite. Fortunately Tracy loved the heat, and didn't suffer from the humidity which caused so much of the population to flee indoors for the relief that air-conditioners could afford them.

The house was set high on a hilly slope, and below her Tracy saw the myriad lights of the city. Especially colourful was the coastal road, with lights twinkling and sparkling in what seemed an unending carnival spirit. Indeed, were she to drive down there now she would find herself mingling with the many tourists thronging the promenades and amusement-parks above the beaches. Further out the Indian Ocean was austerely black against the starlit sky. Here and there were the lights of ships, motionless, each one waiting its turn for a berth in the Durban harbour.

Tracy had always loved this view. Yet tonight she found herself unable to enjoy it.

She would make her way to Ifafa Beach, she decided. Once there she would find out how to get to Umhlowi. She had suggested a phone-call to her sister, but her mother had protested. Allison could be eloquent when she chose, she could talk herself out of most situations. A face-to-face confrontation, and an unexpected one at that, had the most chance of success. Either Allison would be amenable to reason or not, one way or the other Tracy could be back in Durban in a matter of days.

It was strange then that she felt uneasy. As if by going to Umhlowi things would never be quite the same again. It was an uneasiness that she could not explain.

She caught the train the next morning. The undulating sugar-cane covered hills gave way to fruit farms as the train chugged its way southwards. Mangoes, lychees, bananas and pawpaws began to be seen with more frequency. The train was never far from the coast. On one side were the farmlands, on the other the sea. Tracy's co-passengers were enchanted with the views that unfolded at every turn of the railway-line, but she herself was preoccupied.

It was strange, she thought, she was going on a journey to save her sister from a too-hasty marriage. At the same time she was putting distance between herself and a man who wanted to marry her, delaying the making of a decision, so that in a way a few days away from home were a relief of a sort.

And yet the uneasiness persisted. At Ifafa Beach she got off the train. How to proceed from the seaside village? she wondered. On the assumption that a local estate agency would be familiar with most of the farms in the district, she walked into the nearest one and asked for directions.

There was a bus that stopped not far from Umhlowi, said the man who answered her query, but a taxi would probably be her best bet at this particular hour of the day. He showed no surprise at the name of the farm, which was reassuring. For the first time Tracy acknowledged the suspicion that she had thought she might arrive here only to find that the name Derrick Demant had given had been a fictitious one.

The taxi drove along the coastal road a few miles before turning inland, and Tracy began to take an interest in her surroundings. The countryside was so lush and profuse. Set back from the road were the disciplined lands of the fruit-farms, but closer at hand there was just profuse vegetation and colour. All along the railway tracks there had been palm-trees, pawpaw and banana palms growing wild as weeds, and here beside the road there were even more palms. There were no spaces between them, there was just a riotous undergrowth of a fleshý-leafed plants and brightly coloured shrubs, a few shoots of wild sugar-cane here, a scarlet poinsettia or hibiscus that had seeded itself there. All of it strong and hardy beneath the hot African sun.

They came at last to Umhlowi, and Tracy sat straighter in her seat as the taxi-driver left the car to open a pair of great wrought-iron gates set beneath a tall stone archway. Her interest deepened as they proceeded along a drive that was bordered by scarlet-flowered flame-trees. Through the flame-trees she could see the orchards. Row upon row of fruit-trees, citrus and mangoes, extending as far as the eye could see, healthy-looking and with the appearance of being carefully tended. None of the riotous undergrowth here that she had seen on the highway. It would take much discipline to keep it at bay, she realised, and understood that Umhlowi was a much more impressive place than either she or her mother had anticipated.

At the farmhouse, a lovely white-walled building surrounded by great shady trees, the taxi came to a halt. Tracy paid the driver and experienced a moment of panic. Was she crazy to have come all this way? Would she get any sympathy from the people who lived here? Perhaps they would feel that any mess Allison and her Derrick had got into was of their own making. But the panic was momentary. She had come here for a purpose and she was not going to let the grandeur of Umhlowi and the possible uninterest of its owners deter her. She watched the vehicle drive away. Then she lifted her chin and made for the big oak door.

A finger was on the bell, ready to press it, when she heard the sound. A wailing sound, constant and piteous. She saw the cat almost immediately. It was in a tree, and it was looking down at her, its mouth opening in one long unhappy mew after another.

'Poor thing, you're stuck!' Tracy exclaimed. And then, stepping nearer, 'Why, you're just a scrap of a kitten.'

In a moment she had kicked off her open sandals, and was shinning up the tree with all the expertise of the tomboy she had once been. The kitten stopped its mewing at her approach. It was further up than she had realised, but she climbed within reach of it, stretched out a hand and plucked it from the niche of a forked branch.

'There,' she said gently, stroking the soft fur. 'You're safe now.'

Going up had been relatively easy. The way down, Tracy realised all too quickly, was not going to be easy at all. She could have done with an extra foothold. Cradling the kitten against her, she pondered her course of action.

'In a bit of a fix are you?' a vital voice asked.

Tracy's heart gave a little jerk as she glanced into the most arresting male face she had ever seen. It was lean and tanned and rugged, with skin that was stretched tightly over high cheekbones. Beneath thick winging brows the eyes were dark and intelligent, and the chin had a very firm line to it. There would be arrogance in the face, she thought, but at this moment there was only amusement.

'I *am* in a fix,' she acknowledged ruefully, wondering how long he had been watching her.

'For starters you could pass me the kitten.'

She reached down to him. As he took the kitten his

fingers touched hers, and the strangest tingling shot
through her hand. Almost as if she had been burned,
she thought confused. The kitten was dropped lightly
to the ground and a moment later it had scampered
away in the direction of the house.

'Your turn,' said the man.

'I can manage,' Tracy said quickly.

'Can you?' There was a glimpse of strong teeth as
his lips lifted in a grin.

She couldn't do it, of course. She had known that in
the moment before she had seen him. But for some
reason the thought of his help sparked off a core of
defiance. Unsuccessfully she edged a foot along the
trunk.

'There seems to be a foothold missing,' she said at
length, ruefully.

'I'll arrange to have one installed before you climb
the tree again,' he drawled.

She was suddenly breathless. She would have to let
him help her. Bad enough if she had been wearing
jeans, but she had on a sundress and her legs were
bare. He was watching her, a glint in his eyes. He
knew she was uncomfortable, and the knowledge gave
him satisfaction. Her eyes met his and colour washed
her cheeks. He would help her, but he would take his
sweet time about it.

Lazily he reached up. Long fingers, as tanned as his
face, touched her legs, sliding towards her thighs. It
was the only way to get her out of the tree, she
acknowledged that through the pounding in her head,
but did the procedure have to be quite so sensuous?
Or was the sensuousness merely a product of her own
overworked imagination?

The hands on her thighs tightened, helping her to
descend to the nearest foothold. Then his hands
slipped to her waist and he was lifting her the rest of
the way.

'Thank you,' she said jerkily as her feet touched the ground.

'The pleasure was entirely mine.' He was laughing at her, the dark eyes were wicked and he was still holding her.

Feeling flustered and vulnerable, she moved out of his hands. Wretched kitten, it had spoiled her dignified arrival at Umhlowi. 'Well . . . thank you,' she said again, because she did not know what else to say.

The man was regarding her with interest.

'You didn't come here just to rescue a cat. Suppose you tell me who you are and why you're here.'

She decided to take the second question first. 'I'm looking for Mr Demant.'

'You're looking right at him.'

She stared at him in amazement. 'That's impossible!'

Dark eyes held a fresh glimmer of amusement. 'I assure you I know who I am.'

She shook her head, confused. 'You're not at all like your photo.'

An eyebrow rose. 'You've seen a photo of me?'

'Just yesterday.'

'And I don't resemble it?'

She'd taken the person in the photo to be about the same age as herself. Not long out of boyhood. This was a man, a real man in every sense of the word. There was strength and power in every well-built inch of him. There was also a rugged sexuality coupled with a kind of all-encompassing maleness. Dynamic was the word that flashed to mind.

'You're older for one thing.' She had waited just a moment too long to answer him, and she knew he had registered her confusion.

'You have me intrigued.' He was eyeing her speculatively now. 'You haven't told me who you are.'

'My name is Tracy Galland.'

'Galland!' The last traces of amusement left his face. 'A name I know.'

She met his gaze squarely. 'I'm sure you do. I'm Allison Galland's sister. We want her back, Mr Demant.'

'Take her any time you choose,' he said drily.

He had tired of her quickly. Which was not altogether surprising, Tracy thought. She could see why Allison would have fallen for him. It would be difficult to find the woman who could remain unaffected by this man's spectacular good looks. But it was harder to understand why he would be attracted to a girl as young as Allison. She could not see them as a couple. Husband and wife, sharing a lifetime together.

'You don't want her?' she asked.

'Absolutely not.'

'Pity you didn't make it clear how you felt,' Tracy said with some asperity. 'You'd have saved Allison a lot of unhappiness and me the inconvenience of a trip down here.'

A cynical gaze flicked her face. 'And you think your sister would have listened to me?'

'No point in eloping if one of the parties is unwilling,' Tracy said.

There was a moment of silence, and then Mr Demant gave a roar of laughter. The sound was no less attractive than Tracy would have pictured it to be. Vital and low and as sexy as the rest of him. 'You think I plan to marry that silly girl?'

Tracy took a step backwards. 'So you just wanted her as your mistress . . .'

'Miss Galland . . .'

In her anger she did not hear him cut in. 'You're even lower than I'd imagined. Fortune-hunting would have been bad enough if your intentions had been honourable. I suppose you found a way of getting every last penny out of Allison, and now you want to abandon her.'

'Your sister,' he said conversationally, 'is a bundle of trouble. But *you* are a termagant.'

She took a breath. 'Only when I'm roused.'

'You rouse easily.' There was a sudden gleam in his eyes. 'Are you as easily aroused in other ways?'

No mistaking what he was getting at. 'How dare you!' she accused furiously.

'You'd be surprised—pleasantly perhaps.' The words were all the more outrageous for the mildness with which they were spoken. 'Like to give it a try?'

'Just call my sister,' she ordered through clenched teeth, 'and then we'll leave.'

'Impossible.'

She stared at him. 'Why?'

Dark eyes were mocking. 'A case of mistaken identity for one thing.'

She felt suddenly unsure of herself. 'You said your name was Demant.'

'So it is. Ryan Demant. I believe the man whose blood you're after is my brother, Derrick.'

Ryan Demant? Her mother had said nothing about a brother. A brother who was arrogant and sexy, and better-looking than most film-stars.

Dimly she was aware that she had made herself look somewhat foolish. Perhaps it was too late to remedy the situation. Nevertheless she lifted her chin and said quietly, 'I did make a mistake, I'm sorry. Would you call Derrick, please? And Allison too?'

Again his eyes ran over her. Tracy wished she could read the expression in them. 'They're not within calling distance.'

She was about to ask where they were, when Ryan said, 'Tell me why you consider my brother to be a fortune-hunter.'

'We'd come into money, my sister and I.'

'So you are a couple of heiresses?'

'Only in a manner of speaking.'

She looked at him, wondering whether to go into specifics. It was really none of his business. On the other hand, she had no way of knowing just what Allison had told Derrick. The word heiress was inappropriately grand to the circumstances. If Ryan, and through him Derrick, were to learn the truth, there might still be hope.

'An uncle left us some money. Five thousand each,' she said matter-of-factly.

There was another burst of laughter. 'I would think that would buy at least two wheels of the Ferrari Derrick was planning to buy himself.'

The truth hit her quite suddenly, leaving her stunned. She looked at the lovely farmhouse, at the lush spread of orchards. Very carefully she said, 'This is Derrick's home?'

Mocking eyes were unmerciful. 'Isn't that why you came here?'

'Yes . . .' She stopped, confused. This arrogant man knew exactly what had gone through her mind, he did not need answers to his questions, but he enjoyed playing with her.

'You thought that Derrick was a rather penniless farmworker on the look-out for a quick penny?'

'Something like that,' she admitted.

Ryan Demant pushed his hands into the pockets of well-cut brown cords. 'Derrick and I farm Umhlowi together.'

To her horror Tracy felt a blush warm her face. There was nothing she could do to stop it, and she knew that Ryan had seen it, for the mocking expression was intensified. She should have known the truth the moment she'd seen this man. No matter that his clothes were casual. He had the peculiar aura of power and easy confidence that belonged to the very rich.

'I suppose,' he said now, 'knowing that Derrick is not the fortune-hunter you thought him makes a difference?'

She looked up quickly to find dark eyes searching her face. 'Not a bit,' she answered without hesitation.

His expression altered. Ryan Demant had the look of a man who had been surprised.

'*Should* it make a difference?' Tracy asked.

'My brother,' Ryan said drily, 'is quite a wealthy man. To most women that seems to make all the difference in the world.'

You've been hurt, Tracy thought. There have been women who have been interested in you only for your money.

She lifted her chin. 'I don't think it would make a difference to Allison. I know it would mean nothing to me.'

His glance swept her, taking in the piquant face with its lovely cheekbones and almond-shaped green eyes, the cloud of fair hair and the lips that lifted generously at the corners. It was a glance from which Tracy would have liked to look away, and yet she found she could not move her eyes from Ryan's.

Striving for a calmness she did not feel, she said, 'Tell me how to find Allison.'

'I thought we'd established it was not possible.'

'I must find my sister.'

'She is not at Umhlowi.'

Panic welled inside Tracy. 'Is it too late? They've really run off together?'

Ryan shrugged.

'Oh my God!' Slender shoulders drooped a little. Tracy had been so sure that this was one more scrape Allison had got herself into, never meaning it to be permanent. Now it seemed she had been wrong.

CHAPTER TWO

'I'M wondering why you're quite so upset,' Ryan said.

'Apart from the fact that my mother will probably have a heart attack over this, Allison's too young, Mr Demant. All very well that Derrick swept her off her feet but they hardly know each other. It can't work.'

'Bit late to think about that. They've fled the nest.'

'And very satisfied you are about it too,' she said on a sudden surge of anger.

'Wrong. I'm damn annoyed.'

She was taken aback. 'You are?'

The dark eyes flicked her face, mocking her astonishment. 'You think you're the only one against the union?'

'What are your reasons?' she asked after a moment.

'Derrick took off at a bad time. We're up to our ears in work right now, he knew that, and yet he decided to have a romance with a silly little girl.'

It was one thing for Tracy to think of Allison as silly and with no thought for the consequences of her actions. It was quite another for this arrogant Ryan Demant to criticise her sister.

'You're very rude.' She threw the words at him.

'Just telling you how I see it. Your sister put out her claws to catch Derrick. Not the first one, I may say, but the first to succeed.'

'And Derrick had no hand in the matter I suppose,' she countered evenly, trying to hold on to her temper.

'Derrick has always liked pretty girls,' said his brother. 'Doesn't take much for him to be infatuated. But this is the first time he's thought of getting married.'

'Why do I get the feeling you hold Allison responsible?'

'I think she seduced him.'

'That's outrageous!' Without thinking, she lifted her hand to wipe the contemptuous expression from his face.

He caught her hand before it could meet its target. 'You've quite a temper, haven't you?' He laughed. 'Wait for me to qualify my words before you get violent.'

The hand on her wrist burned the delicate skin. She could feel every one of the long fingers, making her shiver. Dean had done a great deal more than touch her hand and she had never reacted this way. It was absurd that she could let this arrogant man get to her like this.

'Start qualifying,' she snapped.

'I wasn't talking about physical seduction.'

His eyes sparkled dangerously and his lips were slightly lifted at the corners.

'What other kind of seduction is there?' she demanded.

'Psychological. More potent every time, Miss Galland, as I'm sure you know.' He looked at her. 'Or haven't you tried it?' he added insolently.

She pulled her wrist from his hand. 'Just get to the point.'

'Your sister is a pretty girl. Shrewd too. She saw the effect she had on Derrick, and played on it. Held out for marriage.'

'*I* wouldn't let a man make love to me unless we were married.' Tracy didn't know what made her say it. She felt a little foolish, but now that the words were out she could hardly take them back or explain them.

'You wouldn't?' Slowly Ryan Demant's eyes travelled over her, lingering for an interminable moment on her lips before travelling downwards. She could actually feel his eyes on her throat, on her breasts, on the slim waist and the slender legs which he had already touched with his hands. Colour flared once more in her cheeks and she had to curl her fingers hard into her palms in order to keep some measure of composure.

'We were talking about Allison,' she reminded him.

'Ah.'

'Are they married?'

'Not yet.'

'Thank God!' She was so relieved that she forgot her outrage. 'Are you sure? How do you know?'

'I overheard them talking. Seems it's about a month to your sister's eighteenth birthday.'

'I thought they would lie about her age.'

'In that they're showing more sense than you gave them credit for. No, they want no legal problems.'

'Then why did they leave here?'

Ryan chuckled. 'Perhaps because they guessed that you might follow them and try to put a stop to things.'

'Then there's still hope.'

He shrugged. 'If you say so.'

'We have to go after them.'

His eyebrows rose. 'Have to?'

'You dislike the thought of this marriage as much as I do.' She was pleading with him now, and was not ashamed of it. 'Please, Mr Demant, let's go after them.'

'I can't.'

Tracy tried to push aside a feeling of helplessness. 'You don't know where they've gone?'

After a moment he said, 'I know.'

'Then there's no problem.'

'Not in your eyes perhaps.' His voice was level. 'I've already told you this is a busy time for us here at Umhlowi. Derrick's gone just when I needed him most. Means I'll have to do his work as well as my own.'

What did it take to get through to the man? 'Doesn't

it mean anything to you that this whole affair is a disaster?'

The eyes on her face were impersonal. 'I think you're over-dramatising.'

Tracy drew a deep breath. 'I promised my mother I would get Allison back. You know where she is.'

'But I'm not going after them.'

'Is there no way I can persuade you?' Tracy asked, feeling a little desperate.

In the silence that followed the question she was swept with a sense of sheer frustration. Lucille had thought Tracy had only to go to Umhlowi for Allison to be returned to the maternal haven, as safe and as virginal as she had left it. Lucille would not be able to conceive of the man who stood beneath the cloudless African sky, more self-assured and implacable than anyone Tracy had ever met.

She turned away from him, her eyes taking in the fruit-trees that stretched to the horizon and beyond. 'Is there no way?' she asked again.

'Perhaps,' he said at length.

'Then you *will* consider following them?' she burst out gladly, swinging round to look at him. 'Why don't we set out right away?'

He made a gesture. 'Not so fast. What I'm considering is a deal.'

'I don't think I understand.' She looked at him uncomprehendingly.

'It's really quite simple. This little escapade has meant double work for me. You do Derrick's share and then I'll lead you to the happy pair.'

There was a wicked sparkle in the brown eyes. He was holding a gun to her head, and they both knew it.

'How long would this—deal—last?'

'Allison's birthday is in a month.'

'You wouldn't expect me to be here that long!'

He shrugged. 'Take it or leave it.'

His expression was relentless, but she met his gaze unflinchingly. 'When do I start?'

For a second there was something in his face that could have been admiration. Then he said impassively, 'Tomorrow.'

'What will I be doing?'

'I'll explain as we go along.'

She looked down at her suitcase. 'I'll need somewhere to stay.'

He gestured towards the lovely farmhouse. 'You'll stay right here.'

'Your wife won't mind?'

'I'm not married.'

She tried to ignore the sensation, the quite unexpected sensation of pleasure. Why on earth should it matter to her if Ryan Demant was married or not!

She shook her head. 'In that case I can't stay here.'

'Old-fashioned are you?' he drawled.

She refused to rise to the bait. 'Do you have a live-in housekeeper?'

After a second he said, 'No.'

'Then I'll stay in the village.'

'How did you get here?'

'By train. I caught a taxi to Umhlowi.'

'I thought I didn't see a car. So the village won't do. We start work at daybreak.'

'I'll be here.'

'The bus that goes this way leaves later.'

And a daily taxi was more than she could afford. There was Uncle Ned's legacy, of course, but she had other plans for that.

'I can't stay in the house with you.' She pushed a wave of hair from her forehead. 'You must see that, Mr Demant.'

'Ryan. And from this point on I'll call you Tracy. Since we're going to be living together there's no point in standing on ceremony.'

Her temples were pounding. 'We are not going to be living together.'

'Do you suppose I meant in the physical sense?'

Something in his expression seemed to imply that he had meant just that.

'You must see how impossible it is,' she said helplessly.

'I only know that unless you fill in for Derrick we won't be catching up with your sister.'

Did you envision this kind of trap when you sent me out here, Mother?

'There *must* be some other way,' she said a little desperately.

'Your young sister had no qualms about running off with Derrick. Sharing very limited quarters along the way. Yet you need a chaperon in a house filled with rooms. Are you frightened of me, Tracy?'

Yes, she was frightened. The oddest kind of fear. She could not quite put a name to it.

'Of course not,' she snapped with a sureness she was far from feeling. 'Some things are right, that's all.'

He laughed suddenly, and again the sound sent a shiver through her. 'Who would have thought little Allison's sister would be a model of correctness. Tell you what, Tracy, I've just thought of something that might suit you.'

She looked at him eagerly. 'You have?'

'You can't see it from here, but behind the house is the original farmstead. You could stay there.'

'Perfect!' she exclaimed.

'Not all that perfect. It's just a shack. It was built in the days when indoor plumbing was not always part of a house.'

'Meaning?'

'The bathroom facilities are basic to say the least.'

'That doesn't worry me.'

'An outhouse for a toilet, and the bathroom water comes from a rain-water tank.'

'You're not scaring me off.' She was unaware that her eyes sparkled like emeralds, and that her face was suffused with a soft warmth, a combination that made her quite beautiful to the watching man.

'You really are determined to save that silly sister of yours.' His expression was enigmatic, giving away nothing of his thoughts.

'Absolutely.'

Without warning Ryan's hand went to her hair, pushing a damp tendril from her forehead. She could feel his fingers on her face, and lightly, oh so lightly, on the edge of her scalp. Tracy forced herself to stand very still. He dropped his hand. The moment of contact had lasted no more than a few seconds.

Softly Ryan said, 'You're quite a girl. Come inside with me now, and I'll get you something to drink.'

It was a beautiful house, Tracy saw almost at once. The living-room had a huge picture window that took up almost the whole of one wall. A sun-room led off on one side of it, a dining-room on the other. Everywhere were the big windows which gave the house a pervading aura of spaciousness and light.

Fitting in with the general atmosphere, the furniture was long and low and pale-wooded. Carpets and curtains were in muted shades of blue and turquoise which gave just the correct touch of coolness to a house which would be very hot for most of the year. On the walls were some lovely pictures which Tracy would have liked to study more closely. Here and there stood great white tubs of flowering plants, which, when combined with the big windows, had the effect of merging outdoors with indoors.

Aware, quite suddenly, of silence, Tracy turned and looked at the man who had stopped a few paces behind her. He had been watching her, she saw at a glance.

'It's very beautiful,' she said huskily.

'Thank you.'

'I was trying to picture Allison living here.'

'I thought,' he said drily, 'that the object of your mission is to prevent that from happening.'

'So it is,' she agreed, and was glad when he made no further comment on the contrariness of her thoughts but led her to the kitchen instead.

Hardly a bachelor pad, had been her first impression on entering the house. It was an impression that was now reinforced. As neat and brightly spacious as the rooms she had already seen, the kitchen was every housewife's dream. Modern fittings and lots of counter-space, and a big bay window so that a woman could look out over the garden while she prepared a meal. Gnarled-wood cupboard doors and antique copper pots saved the room from being a magazine-picture of efficiency and made it comfortably rustic instead.

'You're sure you're not married?' she asked curiously.

Ryan turned from the fridge from which he was taking lemonade and ice. 'I'd hardly be unsure about a thing like that.'

'Everything's so ... so cared for. Not even a housekeeper, I think you said.'

'Not one who lives in,' he corrected. 'We were talking of chaperons if you remember.' He grinned. 'There is a woman, a very capable woman, who comes in from the village several times a week. Care to help with the fruit, Tracy?'

They would go to the sun-room, he said. He carried a tray with the lemonade and two glasses, and motioned to Tracy to follow with a bowl of peaches and plums and rough-skinned lychees.

Biting into a lychee that was as sweet and cool as ambrosia, Tracy looked through the big window across a colour-filled rose-garden to the orchards beyond. There was a loveliness here that she had not imagined. Again she tried to picture Allison in this setting. She had not changed her mind about finding her sister and taking her back to Durban with her, for an impetuous marriage had to be the surest way of heading for disaster. Yet the thought crossed her mind that Allison, any woman for that matter, would be happy at Umhlowi. With Ryan. Instinctively she looked across at Ryan and in that moment she realised that she had actually associated the man with the setting. He was part of it in a way that Allison and the unknown Derrick were not.

Really, her thoughts made no sense at all, she decided crossly. If Allison were to live here it would be with Derrick. And why Ryan should have entered her mental picture was a mystery she did not care to analyse.

So cross was she with herself, that when they'd finished the last of the lemonade and Ryan murmured softly, 'Care to see the bedrooms now?'

She snapped back, 'I'm in no mood to be seduced.'

'Ah.' She heard the laughter in his throat. 'Did I mention seduction?'

'A while back you did. And when a man tries to get a girl into his bedroom there's just one thing on his mind.'

'Fought back a few men in your time, have you?'

'Always successfully,' she answered him pertly.

'Do you know,' he said lazily, 'I think it might be rather fun to seduce you.'

A little nerve tingled unexpectedly along her spine. 'You'd be wasting your time.'

'Perhaps you're the one who's wasting something. That sexy body of yours looks as if it was made for loving.'

A treacherous voice deep inside her told her that he was probably right. Tracy got to her feet and made to pick up the tray. 'This, I think, can go back to the kitchen.'

A hand caught hers before she could make contact with the tray. 'Scared of sex are you, Tracy?'

'Just put off by the one-night stand variety,' she told him, with as much disdain as she could summon over the pulsing of her senses.

A thumb stroked her wrist, slowly, sensuously, sending ripples of awareness along the delicate skin. 'Marriage or nothing for you, was what you said earlier.'

'Exactly.' She managed to pull her wrist from his fingers. 'The tray.'

'Ah yes, the tray. Something might happen to the crockery if it isn't rinsed off immediately.'

He was laughing at her again, but she did not care. Or yes, she did care. But his laughter was preferable to an atmosphere which was making her feel more vulnerable by the minute.

She had not expected him to follow her into the kitchen, but he did. There was no need to turn her head to know quite how near he was to her, she could judge the nearness by the prickling sensation of the hair on the back of her neck. This was absurd, she really would have to get a hold of herself. For a while she would have to see this man every day, and this discomforting feeling of awareness in his presence was no way to begin the relationship.

'I see the sink,' she said politely.

'And you know how to turn on the water.' He laughed again, and she wasn't sure if it was the low seductiveness of the sound or the warm breath fanning her neck which caused her pulses to race.

'Right.' Tracy was no prim miss, but she had an idea that a prim tone was called for now.

'Right,' he mocked her. 'You wash, lady, I'll dry.'

'I'll manage.'

'This isn't part of Derrick's chores.'

'I realise that . . .'

'Why not co-operate, Tracy? Then we can get out and enjoy the day.'

She looked at him. 'We?'

A patrician eyebrow lifted. 'You've someone else you'd rather spend it with?'

He was standing so close to her that she was conscious of every long inch of him. He was leaning against the kitchen table, one leg stretched carelessly across the other, his eyes sparkling as they studied her. He was seeing right through her clothes, she understood that, and he was making no effort to hide his enjoyment.

It was the arrogant sparkle in the dark eyes that made her say tartly, 'Quite a few—but not in this particular neck of the woods.'

'A special boyfriend?'

Was Dean special? No, said a part of her that yearned for excitement, and yes, passion, before she settled down with a husband.

None of which she could say to Ryan. She merely shrugged.

Something flickered in the dark eyes. Casually he said, 'Might as well spend the day together in that case.' He picked up a tea towel. 'Well, are you going to wash?'

Abruptly she tore her eyes away from the virile figure. As she turned on the taps, she thought that such was the measure of his masculinity that a tea towel looked not the slightest bit incongruous in his hands.

'We'll go sailing,' he informed her.

She swung round. 'Sailing!'

'Scared of that too?'

'Oh no!' She smiled at him.

'I take it the answer is yes.' Dark eyes on her face were intent.

'I'd love to go sailing.'

The thought popped into her mind that the idea of spending the day with him, whatever the activity, was appealing.

'What do I wear?'

He laughed. 'Why is that the first question a woman asks in any situation? Brought a swimsuit?'

She shook her head, disappointed. 'I didn't plan on staying. I just have a few basic necessities.'

'Doesn't matter. I think I know where to find a bikini.'

It didn't take long to wash up. Yet there are actions which cannot be measured in terms of time. Given the right circumstances even minutes could be meaningful, Tracy decided, with a quick glance at the handsome man who was drying the dishes. In Ryan's hands the chore took on panache. But then most things he did would have panache.

Minutes, that was all they spent in the kitchen together, and spent on the most mundane of things. But perhaps it was the very mundaneness that made Tracy able to relax for the first time in the presence of a man who, for all his attractiveness, was also intimidating. She relaxed enough to try to picture Dean in the kitchen of her flat in Durban—and failed. Dean, darling though he was, was at all times conscious of his male dignity. He would never unbend as this man did.

'Why the smile?' she heard Ryan ask.

It would be disloyal to tell him her thoughts. 'Just looking forward to the day,' she told him.

'And do your lips always look so kissable when you smile?'

Involuntarily the smile widened. 'Mr Demant, may I remind you of the reason for my presence here?' she said with the mock primness she had affected earlier. 'Why not pretend you're talking to Derrick?'

His eyes sparkled. 'That's asking the impossible. Derrick doesn't come packaged in five feet and about six inches of delectable curves. Nor does he have lips which I happen to find very tempting.'

At the last words his glance had come to rest meaningfully on her mouth, and now he took a step towards her. For a moment Tracy watched him, standing as still as if she was mesmerised, her breath stopped in her throat.

She hesitated a moment, and then catching herself, moved backwards just in time. 'The bikini,' she reminded him a little shakily. 'And if you'll take me to the shack I'll get changed.'

'Time to go there later,' he said. 'You can get changed in one of the rooms here.' The sparkle intensified as his eyes travelled over her figure. 'I promise that your privacy won't be invaded.'

Tracy did not change immediately after closing the door of the guest room. She needed a few moments to calm nerves that were surprisingly frenzied. More particularly, she needed time to wonder why she felt quite so rattled. There had been a certain look in Ryan's eyes minutes earlier, when she'd backed away from his kiss. For he *had* been about to kiss her. If she was sure of little else at this moment, she was sure of that. Neither her hesitation nor the too-hasty retreat had escaped him. He had guessed that she had been tempted to let him kiss her, and the knowledge had given him undoubted satisfaction. Which was not strange.

What *was* strange was her own reaction to the man. Tracy hadn't reached the age of twenty-two without boyfriends and kisses. Kisses which for the most part she had enjoyed, though she had never been swept away to the point where she had lost control of a situation. It was not through want of invitation that she had not been to bed with a man. Nor was it merely a question of morals. Rather there was a feeling that she wanted sex, when it happened, to be something special. An act of love to be shared with a man she loved.

She did not love Ryan. It was impossible to love a man she had known less than an hour. And yet in this short space of time something in Tracy's make-up had changed. For the first time in her life she had experienced a sharp desire to be in a man's arms. A desire that was physical and totally unexpected. A desire that went beyond kisses. She hadn't known that she could feel this way about a man she hardly knew and wasn't even sure she liked. It was the strangest feeling, unsettling, and yet while it lasted it had been delightful too. Now that it was over she felt shaken.

She was behaving like a teenager on a first date, she thought as she unzipped her dress. Worse than a teenager. She was a mature woman and should know that chemistry could do strange things. Time to get a grip on her feelings, she reminded herself, not for the first time. And it would be a good idea to remember that Ryan Demant was a very physical man, one who liked women and who took his fun where he could get it.

The bikini was a pale gold colour. Two tiny pieces of fabric, seductively designed and skimpier than any bikini Tracy had ever owned. It fitted her though it was a little loose for her in places. The woman who owned it must be bigger-breasted, bigger-hipped than Tracy herself. A slender woman, yet voluptuous. And sensuous. Only a sensuous woman would have chosen this particular scrap of allure.

Tracy stood before a full-length mirror and saw that the bikini did more for her than anything she possessed. It emphasised the sleekness of her waist and thighs, and enhanced the curves of a very feminine figure. Her cheeks warmed to the knowledge

that Ryan would see her like this, and she did not
know if she was glad of the fact or not.

From tomorrow she would wear the working clothes
of a man, she would be dressed like a man. And if she
did the work to Ryan's satisfaction then he would take
her to Allison in time to stop the marriage. From
tomorrow she would, to all intents and purposes, be
another Derrick. But today she was Tracy. A female.
And in this bikini she was more female than she had
ever suspected she could be. She knew suddenly that
yes, she *was* glad that on this one day Ryan would see
her purely as a woman.

As she put her sun-dress in her case and pulled
jeans and a blouse on over the bikini, her thoughts
went back to its owner. Not Ryan's wife, if she was to
believe that he was not married. A sister perhaps? Had
Derrick mentioned a sister? Her mother knew
amazingly little about Derrick Demant, if there was a
sister Allison might never have mentioned the fact.

If there was no sister, then that left only a girlfriend.
Which was not surprising. There would be many
women in Ryan's life, and the fact did not concern her in
the least. That it should have given her even the slightest
moment for pause was irrational she decided firmly.

Ryan was waiting for her outside the farmhouse. He
had changed too, and in a chest-hugging navy T-shirt
and shorts, clothes which showed the long tanned
body to good advantage, he looked even more dynamic
than before. He had brought the car to the front of the
house. Seating herself beside him Tracy found herself
once more acutely aware of him.

They talked as he drove, easy conversation, which
was just as well, for Tracy's mind was operating on
two levels. There was the one that supplied light
responses to Ryan's questions; and there was the one
that took in the tautness of the tanned legs and arms,
and the deep lines that ran upwards from the corners

of his lips, and the laughter lines around his eyes. She thought of the moment when he had come close to kissing her, and she remembered the sensuousness of her own body in the borrowed bikini, and the muscles of her stomach tightened with sudden anticipation. She had a feeling that this was going to be a day she would not easily forget.

CHAPTER THREE

IT was a day made for sailing. On board the *Seagull* Tracy looked around her in delight. Craft of all kinds rode the waves. Motor-boats and small yachts and spinnakers with brightly coloured sails. The sky was cloudless and the slight breeze made for a gentle sea.

For the first twenty minutes or so Ryan had been occupied with the business of getting the yacht away from its moorings and well beyond the breakers. He came to her now, and she saw that he had shed his outer clothes. In a pair of white trunks he looked so stunning that she sucked in her breath. Did Derrick have the same appeal as his brother? Until now she had been merely exasperated with Allison, but she was beginning to realise that her sister might have been overwhelmed by feelings that were too strong for a young girl to fight.

'You look a trifle overdressed,' Ryan said.

She smiled at him, wondering if he had any inkling of the effect he was having on her, thankful that she was able to keep her voice light. 'There's a dress-code on the high seas?'

'You're scared again, aren't you?' The deepening grin told her that he was not fooled by her lightness. 'Is shyness another one of your traits?'

Only shyness before Ryan she thought. Dean had seen her many times in a bikini and it had never bothered her. Yes, she was shy now, but she did not want Ryan to know it.

'I'm comfortable,' she told him.

'You could be a lot more comfortable.'

He knew she was wearing the bikini. The sooner she shed jeans and blouse the better, procrastination would only make for embarrassment.

He was watching her as she undressed. She tried to make her movements casual, but she could feel his eyes on her body, and there was a jerkiness in the hands that undid zip and buttons. With unusual care she folded her clothes and put them aside, glad of a few moments to keep her eyes concealed. At last she looked at him bravely.

He was studying her, his expression assessing and thoroughly male. 'Very nice,' came his comment.

'As nice as the person who owns this?' She did not know what had made her say it, except perhaps that she wanted some kind of reassurance.

He had been studying her, his gaze lingering unabashed on the soft curve of breasts only partially covered by the skimpy bikini, moving to the flat midriff and hips, and then downward over her thighs. Now he laughed softly, and as he lifted his head the gleam in dark eyes told her that he understood her feelings. Probably, she realised disconcerted, he understood them a little too well.

'Just as nice,' he acknowledged.

He could, of course, have said 'nicer', but Tracy sensed that he was not given to hollow flattery. Recalling the vision she had conjured up of the bikini's owner, she decided to accept the compliment with grace.

'I'm thirsty,' she said after a moment.

The dark eyes were on her lips. 'I am too.'

He was nothing but a flirt. And yet his outrageousness made it difficult for her to suppress a smile. 'Lemonade,' she said firmly, knowing that he had brought some on board. 'I'll get it.'

'I'll get it for you. And a beer for myself at the same time.'

She watched him walk away, bronzed and muscular, and with a gracefulness that was particularly male. And she wondered how it would feel to be kissed by him. Not just kissed. How it would be to make love with him. She did not wonder if it would be exciting, instinctively she knew that it would be. But she wondered whether coupled with passion there would also be tenderness.

With a little shake of her head she turned and looked out to sea. A spinnaker was skimming the water not far from the *Seagull*; above the roar of the surf she could hear the sound of laughter and shouted words. But she did not try to hear what was said. Her thoughts were taken up with Ryan, and with the situation she had landed herself in. Things were moving too fast. Ryan's behaviour was outrageous, but he was not the first man to make advances to her. What concerned her was her own feelings. She had been attracted to men before now, but never so strongly, and certainly never so fast.

In a way she had preferred him the way he'd been earlier. The man she'd fenced with, the Ryan Demant who'd displayed such arrogance on discovering that she was Allison's sister. He had been easier to cope with then.

He came back to her, and as he handed her a glass of lemonade his fingers touched hers, and the sensation that flamed up her wrist and arm was not unlike the one she'd experienced when he'd touched her thighs. She wondered if the contact had been deliberate.

'Enjoying yourself?' he asked when she'd finished her drink.

She turned a smiling face his way. 'Loving it.'

'You won't love it if you get sunburnt.' He stood up and dropped a bottle of suntan-oil on to her bare-thighed lap. 'Put on some of this stuff.'

She waited a few moments before complying. He went to the wheel of the boat, and then she opened the bottle and squeezed some oil into the palm of one hand. The sun shone savagely out of a cloudless sky, and the reflection of the water was brilliant. It was true that she would get burned if she did not protect herself. She had rubbed the oil into her legs and hips and tummy, and was starting on her shoulders when Ryan returned to her.

'I'll do your back,' he said as he took the bottle out of her hand.

She stifled the protest that came to her lips. Knowing she could not reach her back by herself, Ryan was being helpful. It would seem childish to refuse him, and childishness was one quality that she did not want to display.

The movement of his hands was slow and rhythmic. Light, yet deliberate. Sensuous, achingly sensuous. She was aware of every one of his fingers as they slid over her, and she knew he was not ignorant of the awareness. It was this knowledge that made her sit very still, though it took great effort to do so. She could not see his face, and she was glad that he could not see hers. It was one thing to find the composure to keep her body still, quite another to keep the turmoil from her eyes.

But for all her control, there came a moment when she couldn't sit still any longer. Every nerve was screaming for a release of some kind. Not a break in contact. If anything she wanted more intense contact. She wanted to turn to him and let him hold her. She had already imagined what it would be like to be kissed by him, now she wanted the experience itself.

Restlessly she shifted beneath his hands. 'That will do,' she ordered through tight lips.

The long hands remained on her back, motionless now. And then the movement started again. Lightly, teasingly.

'Ryan!' The name jerked out on a choked breath.

This time he did remove his hands. She drew a shuddering breath of relief. And then she heard him ask, 'You didn't enjoy it?'

'Enjoy?' She found herself unable to meet his eyes. 'You were just protecting me from the sun.'

His hand came round to catch her chin, cupping it, and then she was being turned to face him. She looked at him, her eyes big and green, yet determinedly brave.

'You don't think that was all I was doing.' His own expression was hard to read.

No point in assuming a rather transparent innocence. 'I do know you were trying to provoke me,' she said steadily.

'Provoke, Tracy?' The corners of his lips lifted, and she could see a gleam of white teeth against the dark tan. 'In that bikini you're the one who's provocative. Or didn't you know?'

She was suddenly breathless. But she lifted her chin at him. 'It was your suggestion that I wear it.'

'Of course. But it was your choice to agree. One glance in the mirror must have shown you the desirable image you presented.'

She remembered only too clearly the image the mirror had shown her. He was hard to argue with. If she came back with some clever repartee—assuming that at that moment she could think of any, which she doubted—his own reponse would be rapier-swift.

'I wanted to go sailing with you,' she said simply. 'That's why I wore the bikini. You know that, Ryan.'

An expression which had suddenly altered, made

her go on. 'Why would I want to provoke you anyway?'

Something came and went in the dark eyes as they swung over her face, and the rugged features looked strangely forbidding.

Then Ryan said, 'There must be very few women who couldn't give you the answer to that question. Most females understand that a sexy body can be the key to the things they want.'

'You're hardly flattering the women you know.'

'One of them is your sister.'

Tracy felt anger flare inside her. 'Leave Allison out of this.'

'Why? Not quite eighteen, and already she's well-versed in the wiles of your sex.'

Two bright spots of colour flamed in Tracy's cheeks. 'Why are you so against Allison?'

He shrugged. 'I'm not against her. I happen to believe that she knew what she wanted and went all out to get it. In that she's no different from most other women.'

Had there been a woman who had hurt him? It was hard to believe that this could be so, for he had the look of a man who was invincible. But appearances could deceive, Tracy knew.

And what of Allison herself? Tracy did not think for a moment that her sister had seduced Derrick into wanting to marry her. A flirt Allison might be, and naive enough to think herself in love with a good-looking man just because he showed interest in her. But a deliberate schemer? No, that was something Tracy did not believe. It was unfortunate that without knowing exactly what had happened at Umhlowi she could not defend her sister from a position of strength.

'Allison's not like that,' she said. 'Neither am I.'

Again the dark-eyed gaze went over her, and Tracy was uncomfortably aware of the near-nudity of her breasts, and of the high cut of the panties that revealed not only her thighs but much of her hips. With a flash of irritation this time, she wondered who had owned the bikini. Was it a woman who'd worn it to make herself more alluring? Which gave rise to the inevitable question—more alluring to whom? To Ryan, of course.

'So you're different from other women,' she heard him say.

'If you're so convinced that we're all out to snare men—then yes, I'm different.'

Her eyes sparkled with challenge and she wondered why she felt quite so defiant. Dean was not averse to making chauvinistic remarks at times, and though she always countered them they never made her so angry.

'In fact,' she went on recklessly, 'I wouldn't want *you* if you were being given away.'

She had the satisfaction of seeing his lips thin. Only momentarily, however, for a moment later he was laughing, and even through her anger Tracy had a gut revelation that he was the most attractive man she was ever likely to meet.

'Lucky I'm not about to be given away, by myself or anyone else. Tell me about yourself, Tracy.'

The shift of mood caught her off-balance, robbing her of her anger and making her feel oddly vulnerable. She did not want to talk about herself, not at this moment. It was enough that Ryan could see too much of her body. She did not want to expose her thoughts and dreams for the future to him as well.

Laughing back at him she said, 'Later,' and then she lay back and closed her eyes and lifted her face to the sun.

Beneath her the surf rolled, and on her skin was the heat of the sun. The fact that she had not allowed herself to be cowed by Ryan gave her a sense of satisfaction, and she relaxed her mouth in a smile.

Ryan Demant was an arrogant man who thought he knew everything about women. It was time at least one woman taught him otherwise.

Her eyes flew open as a mouth closed over hers. She tried to sit up but a hand pushed her gently back and a pair of eyes sparkled down into hers.

'Lying there with that smile on your lips was provocative too, whether you'll admit it or not,' Ryan said on a note of malicious good-nature.

There was no chance to answer him, for already he was moving away. As she watched him go, every nerve quivering inside her, she realised that she had in fact taught him nothing at all.

At sunset they berthed and made their way back to Umhlowi. Tracy followed Ryan into the house.

'I'll find my way to the shack now,' she said, picking up her suitcase.

He took it out of her hand and put it back on the ground. 'After we've eaten. Steak and mushrooms and some French bread strike your fancy?'

She was so hungry that she would have settled for a much simpler meal. He grinned when she told him so. 'I'll see to the steak and the mushrooms. You could make the salad,' he suggested.

When Tracy had changed out of the bikini and back into the dress she had worn earlier, she joined Ryan in the kitchen. Appreciatively she sniffed the smell of grilling steak and began to prepare the green salad. She and Ryan worked well together, she reflected. The salad tossed and ready, she began to lay the table, and saw that Ryan was uncorking the wine. Cutlery suspended in her hands, she stood and watched him a moment, aware suddenly of the atmosphere of domestic intimacy which pervaded the room. An intimacy which could easily become habit, and a most delightful one at that. Which was a reason she must not let it happen, for it would end when her stay at Umhlowi ended—and it was a habit she would miss.

Very deliberately she shifted her eyes from Ryan and put the forks and knives on the table. In more ways than one it was just as well that she was going to sleep in the shack. After tonight she would have to find a way of eating there alone, too.

They lingered over a candle-lit meal, talking as they ate. As if by some kind of tacit agreement, they ignored the subject of Allison and Derrick, and conversation flowed easily, going from books to music to the subject of travel, which it seemed was something they both loved. It was so different from her usual conversation with Dean. There was a verve and sparkle to the talk. She could never anticipate Ryan's comments. She was really interested in hearing his views and he seemed eager to hear hers.

'You were going to tell me about yourself,' he said after a while.

Tracy smiled, unaware that the flickering candles gave golden lights to her eyes and a soft mystery to her face. 'We've been talking for hours.'

Ryan leaned back in his chair, and sipped his wine. 'What do you do when you're not out chasing naughty sisters?'

'Photographic modelling.'

The look he gave her was one of interest. 'Have you ever wanted to do anything else?'

Perceptive man. Tracy looked down, her fingers playing with the stem of her wine-glass. Dean did not know of her dream, even her mother knew nothing about it.

'I've always loved photography. I'd like a chance to be on the other side of the camera.'

'Any particular aspect that appeals to you?'

She looked up, wondering why she could talk to Ryan when she had never felt like talking about her dream to anyone else. 'I would like to do a book on Southern Africa—the whole book, photos and text.'

'Any reason why you shouldn't?' He was watching her intently.

'A matter of economics. It would mean giving up my job for a few months so that I could attend a special art course.' She hesitated a moment before going on. 'A kind of sabbatical. I've never been able to do it. But now there's the inheritance. I've been thinking of using some of the money for that.'

She kept her eyes down, waiting for his reaction. In her mind she could hear what Dean would say. 'All that money on a course when you can use a camera quite well already! Why, Tracy, you could put it towards a house.'

But Ryan said softly, 'Sounds good.'

The note of understanding filled her with warmth, and when she spoke again it was without reserve. 'I'd be fulfilling a dream. Have you ever had a dream, Ryan?'

'I have a dream, Tracy.'

His voice had changed. She looked at him, waiting for him to go on. But he was looking at her in an odd sort of way—a disturbing way—and he remained silent. Suddenly she felt uncertain. She opened her mouth, only to close it again without speaking.

She dropped her eyes to hide her confusion, and wished there was a way of concealing the warmth that had crept into her cheeks. Their plates were both empty, she realised—that way lay rescue.

'I suppose we should do the dishes,' she offered, not quite meeting his gaze.

She heard the bubble of laughter in his throat. 'You must be the cleanest girl I ever met. The dishes will keep till later.' A hand closed over hers. 'Bring your wine, we'll go the library.'

She hadn't been in the library until now. She stood

in the doorway a moment looking around her, and thought it must be one of the loveliest rooms she had seen. Bookcases lined two of the walls, books with worn covers that had the look of having been read often. One wall was hung with impressionist-style paintings. French doors filled the fourth wall, and though it was nearly dark Tracy saw that the view looked over the orchards. In a corner was a stereo, and a pair of two-seater settees stood within easy reach of lamps and records.

Turning, she saw that Ryan was watching her, he knew she had caught the atmosphere of the room. 'Like to choose a record?' he suggested.

She sat down on one of the two-seaters, put the wine-glass on the little table beside her, and bent to look through the record collection. The selection was varied, much of it was music she enjoyed, some of it she did not know. She chose a guitar recording, held it out to Ryan and sat back. She was feeling pleasantly tired after the hours in the sun, and the music would make a nice background for their talking.

Moments later the soft strumming of a guitar filled the room, and Ryan came to sit beside her, bringing his wine with him. Somehow she had imagined that he would sit opposite her in the other settee. Momentarily she stiffened. And then she forced herself to look away from his thighs, taut even through his trousers and so close to her own, and tried to concentrate on the congenial air of warmth and cosiness that pervaded the room.

'You got burnt today,' he said after a while.

She danced him a smile. 'Through the suntan-oil?'

'There were parts you neglected.'

'Such as?'

She saw the gleam in his eyes, and wondered what outrageous remark was forthcoming. But no words crossed his lips. Instead he leaned forward, and then she felt the tip of a tongue in the hollow at the base of her throat.

The action was so unexpected, and so devastatingly sensuous, that something exploded inside her, and within moments her body was aflame with desire. In an instinctive defence against her feelings she tried to move away, but the settee held her on one side, and as she tried to get to her feet an arm went around her shoulders, keeping her down.

'Ryan, no,' she protested.

'Yes, Tracy.' His voice was husky and his breath fanned her cheek. 'We've both been wanting it for hours.'

She *had* been wanting it. While they had talked and laughed, while they had been busy with the boat and then the meal, in some corner of her mind she had wondered all the while how it would feel to make love with him. There had been no moment when she had not been aware of him. It was the very depths of the awareness which frightened her.

She tried to move away again, wanting to examine her feelings before she gave in to them. But he was quicker than she was, stronger too.

The weight of his body lay against her as he pressed her gently back against the sofa, and his mouth kissed the spot where his tongue had played.

She was filled with sensation, aching yet delightful. She closed her eyes and curled her hands into tight fists on either side of her lap, almost as if to prove, both to Ryan and herself, that the contact meant nothing to her. As if to pretend to herself that this wasn't really happening.

But it *was* happening. And it did mean something, she acknowledged with a little sigh of pleasure when Ryan's head moved upwards, and his lips began to trace a pattern around hers. The kiss on the yacht had been a playful thing. This was playful too, but in a different way. Lightly, tantalisingly, the lips made a pathway around her mouth, promising but never giving, until she ached with the longing to pull the dark head against her in a deep, mutually satisfying embrace.

His head lifted, and she opened her eyes, and found him watching her, his own eyes intent on her face. Reading her, Tracy thought, and wondered if he knew how he had aroused her. Yes, he did know she realised as she looked back at him, taking in the hard-planed face and the tanned skin and the laughter lines around his mouth, and she was as unable to control her expression as she was to look elsewhere.

He made a little sound in his throat, and then he was bending towards her again. Now his tongue found the contours of her cheeks and eyes—as if he was learning the shape of her face by taste and touch—and then it moved to an earlobe, teasing it, before he caught the soft skin between his teeth. The breath jerked in Tracy's lungs, and now she was no longer able to control herself. The fists unclenched and she brought her hands to his head, burying themselves in his hair, drawing him closer against her.

She heard the swift intake of breath, and then he was rolling backwards, pulling her with him, so that he was against the sofa and she was on top of him. There was nothing teasing in the lips that kissed her now, just a passion that was searching and urgent, kindling such a response in her that it drowned out any shyness as she responded with an ardour of her own. Her lips opened willingly to his, letting him explore the sweetness of her mouth.

When the zip of her dress was pulled down she gave a gasp of surprise, but she did not resist him. And then he was sliding the dress from her shoulders so that his hands could move on her back, and at the touch of the long fingers on her sun-warmed skin a shudder of delight trembled through her. He must have registered her reaction for he kissed her even more deeply, more erotically than before. And she pushed her hands between their bodies, so that she could slide them in turn under his shirt and learn the shape of the hard chest where the heart thudded beneath her fingers.

He pushed the dress further from her body, and she didn't care. All that mattered was that these moments go on, that she could unbutton his shirt and feel the heat of his skin directly against her own.

He paused to breathe, and bringing his hands up to cup her head he held her a little away from him, just far enough so that he could look into her face.

'You're really something,' he said huskily.

So are you, she was about to say, you're like no man I've ever met. I didn't know lovemaking could be like this.

She opened her lips to speak, but the words were delayed as one long finger reached up to trace the corner of her mouth.

'I don't believe Allison could be half as sexy,' he went on.

'Allison?'

She stiffened incredulously as she looked down at him. Why mention her sister at a moment like this?

'I don't believe she could be giving Derrick as much pleasure as you're giving me.'

Feeling suddenly ill, Tracy pushed herself away from him. Ryan tried to hold her back, but anger gave her strength.

'What the hell?' he demanded.

'That's what I should have asked when this started.' Her cheeks were hot, and she felt horribly ashamed that she had given in to him so easily. 'This isn't some contest, Ryan.'

His eyes had narrowed, he was watching her intently. 'Did I say it was?'

'You didn't have to. A few minutes more and you'd have tried to get me to bed, wouldn't you?'

'And you'd have come.' His tone had turned mocking. 'Don't deny it.'

He was right of course. She would have gone to bed with him and the lovemaking would have been beautiful and exciting, and it would have seemed to have a rightness that would have allowed no room for remorse.

But the remorse would have come afterwards, when she'd realised why Ryan had wanted to make love to her in the first place. She blessed the impulse that had led him to make the comparison with Allison now rather than later. Pity he hadn't made it even sooner, for he would have saved her the shame and embarrassment that filled her at this moment.

'You're wrong,' she protested over the dryness in her throat.

'Because you're saving yourself for marriage?' he taunted. 'Allison has her way of getting what she wants, and you have yours. Only you forgot your lines a few minutes ago, didn't you, Tracy? You let a streak of honest passion take over for a while.'

'Don't,' she said painfully.

'Why not? Are you just a tease? Is that your particular line?'

She had forgotten how hateful he could be. Earlier, when he'd found out she was Allison's sister, there had been a hint of it, though his words hadn't hurt nearly as much as they did now. Perhaps because she herself had not been so vulnerable.

'I don't have a line,' she said quietly. 'Not that I expect you to believe it.'

The contempt in Ryan's expression made any verbal reply unnecessary. Hurt played with anger inside Tracy, with anger getting the upper hand as she saw his eyes linger insolently on lips that felt swollen, on the throat with the tell-tale pulse, and then on the breasts that had been bared during their lovemaking.

With as much dignity as she could muster she stood up and lifted her dress back over her shoulders, and reached behind her to do up the zip. She drew her fingers through her hair, then gave up the attempt to neaten it when she realised that only a good brushing could do that. As she dropped her fingers they brushed cheeks that were burning to the touch.

If only she could just get up and walk out of this room and never seen Ryan Demant again. But unfortunately it wasn't so easy. There were things to be said, there was a mission that she had come here to achieve.

She looked at Ryan. He had fastened the buttons of his shirt, and he'd gone to sit on the other settee. As if the very idea of sitting beside her was suddenly distasteful.

She wet her lips. 'I'm not a tease.'

Something flickered in his eyes. 'How about an explanation, a convincing one?'

She evaded the question with one of her own. 'Why did you draw a parallel between Allison and myself?'

'You *are* sisters.'

'That doesn't make us alike.'

'No?' he asked conversationally. 'I don't think Allison is averse to Derrick's position in life and the perks that go with it. What are you after, Tracy?'

On her feet in a moment, she stepped towards him and slapped his face. Drawing away she felt a stinging sensation in her fingers, and saw the red mark on Ryan's face.

For a moment a hiss of breath was his only response. And then, as she was making to move away from him, a hand caught her wrist. He jerked her to him, and she tripped and fell against him, so that his thighs were hard against her chest. She tried to move away from him, but he was holding both her hands now, making it impossible for her to lever herself away from him.

'You little hell-cat!'

There was cruel authority in the tone, and she tilted her head to look at him, and her breath felt raw in her throat.

'That's the second time you've tried that stunt. Do it again and I'll retaliate in my own way. No show of coy outrage will save you next time.'

And then he pushed her away from him, abruptly, as if the contact with her sickened him.

When she had her voice under control, she said, 'I'll go to the shack now.'

'So you're staying?'

'I don't seem to have a choice.'

'Quite,' he agreed, looking amused.

Damn him for his arrogance! Driven by some devil that seemed to take the better of her when she was provoked, Tracy asked, 'What if I were to play my cards right—would you install me here too?'

He was very still. The amusement left his face, and the eyes that met hers were intent. 'Is that what you'd like?' he asked very lightly.

To be your mistress? To live with you here as a kept woman, enjoying every luxury in return for my body? No, a thousand times no!

'I would like you in my bed,' he said when she didn't answer. His voice was still light, just as if they were talking of something quite inconsequential, Tracy thought. 'Devious you may be, but you are also warm and passionate. I think you'd be fun to make love with.'

'I would like,' Tracy said very deliberately, 'to go to the shack.'

After a moment Ryan said, 'If that's what you want.'

She stood up. 'It's what I want.'

He stood up too. 'Wait.'

'No.' Every nerve was screaming with tension inside her. She kept her face averted from him.

'I'll walk with you,' he said.

'I prefer to go alone.'

'It's dark.' His voice had hardened. 'I'll show you the way. Your suitcase is in the hall, Tracy. Get it while I find some sheets and blankets.'

The shack wouldn't be a guest room like the one she had changed in. There wouldn't be a bed made up and waiting. Besides, any guest who came to Umhlowi was likely to be a woman, and the room she slept in would be Derrick's or Ryan's. The owner of the bikini for instance.

Tracy pushed the thought firmly from her mind as she went for her suitcase. Ryan joined her minutes later, carrying linen. Without a word he walked out of the house and she followed him.

CHAPTER FOUR

THE African night was hot, sweet and heady with the smell of fruit and tropical shrubs. Too heady, Tracy thought, for the air was heavy with a sensuousness that made jagged nerves feel raw. She was very aware of the tall figure, physically close and yet remote in the silence that had descended between them since their last exchange. She was *too* aware of him, and wished she knew what to do about it. Her head was throbbing, and she put a hand to a temple, glad that he could not see the gesture.

The shack was not all that far from the house, but it was hidden in a tumble of shrubs and trees, and Tracy ackowledged that if Ryan had not been there to show her the way she might not have found it.

'Key's in my pocket,' he said, waiting for her to take it.

His voice was cool and matter-of-fact and it was true that with both hands holding the linen he could not get at the key himself.

Outwardly cool, Tracy slid her fingers into the pocket of Ryan's trousers. Her fingers touched the key, they also made contact with a hard hip-bone. He did not move by so much as an inch, but he'd been aware of the contact, she knew that, and as she brought out her hand she forced herself to meet his eyes with chill indifference.

She unlocked the door, pushed it open, groped for the lightswitch and stepped inside. A shack was all it was, she saw in a glance. Clean enough, but bare of anything but essentials. There was a bed with a rough-looking mattress, a couple of chairs, a rush mat.

'You can still change your mind.' His tone was enigmatic.

Not a chance that she would give him that satisfaction. She'd rather sleep all night on a bed of nails than back down now. 'It isn't a five-star hotel,' she acknowledged coolly, 'but it will be fine all the same.'

He studied her a long moment, and she wondered what he was thinking. But, 'Let's do the bed,' was all he said.

'I can manage, thanks.'

'Suit yourself.' He shrugged and tossed the linen on the mattress.

In the doorway he stopped. 'We start work at six,' he reminded her.

'I hadn't forgotten.'

'See you then.'

He walked out into the darkness, but not before she

had caught the glint in his eyes. Ryan Demant would be no easy task-master, she thought grimly.

After the lovely air-conditioned rooms of the farmstead the shack was hot and musty. While Ryan had been here it had not seemed quite so desolate. His presence—a rather overwhelming male presence that seemed to dominate his surroundings and make them smaller—had at least given the place a sense of life. Now there was just the heat and the mustiness and an oppressive emptiness. The thought of a month in this place was rather awful.

Tracy picked up a sheet. Mustn't let herself get discouraged on her first day, she decided, determined to be positive. This wasn't a life-sentence after all. Just one month. Bathing in what she presumed would be an antiquated rain-water fed tub and using the out-house would be something to laugh about later. She imagined herself telling Dean about her experiences. They would laugh about them together.

She unfolded the sheets, then pushed the bed away from the wall. It would have been quicker and easier if Ryan had helped her, for the mattress had a queer habit of sliding around on the bed when she tried to tuck in the sheets. But she was glad Ryan had not stayed. She had had quite enough of him for one day. Besides, she welcomed the activity. It gave her something to do.

Making a bed, however fastidiously, took only so much time. Then Tracy unpacked, and that too was accomplished in minutes; expecting the trip to be little more than an over-night affair she had brought few things with her. Afterwards, in this place without books or music or scope for any other activity, emptiness crowded in once more, and there were thoughts that could no longer be pushed away.

She was angry with Ryan. Bitterly angry, for he had known all along what he was doing. He had been playing with her, and expert with women that he undoubtedly was, he had scored quite well. Parts of the day came back to her now. The tender playfulness of some of his kisses, the hot passion of others. The sensuous caresses of his hands on her bare skin and the response they had evoked in her. That was what shamed her now, her response. She had never been stirred by a man as she'd been stirred by Ryan. Without too much more persuasion she might have let him take her to his bed. Only the comparison with Allison had stopped her ... She put her hands to burning cheeks and made a strangled sound in her throat.

There had been purpose in everything Ryan had done. He had known that he was arousing her, she had betrayed herself more than once. And he had done it for just one reason. That Derrick and Allison could be genuinely in love, that was something Ryan did not believe. In his eyes Allison was a creature fit only for his contempt. And Tracy was cast in the same out-for-what-she-could-get mould that he had defined for her sister. Everything that had happened today was just his way of proving his theory.

Tracy was finding it hard to breathe. Whether this was due to the mustiness of the shack, or to her anger, she did not know, but she went to the window and tried to open it. It didn't budge. Probably ages since anyone had spent any time in this place, she thought grimly. There had been no cause to open the window, and with disuse it had become stuck. She could go back to the house and ask Ryan to help her, but she would rather sleep airless and die before morning than do that. Determinedly she worked away at the window and had the satisfaction of feeling it give just a little. After one hard shove it was suddenly open.

Taking long breaths of the scented night air she stood looking out into the darkness. Now that she could breathe she felt a little better, but not much. She was still angry. Angry with Ryan. A perverse kind of anger with Allison for getting her into this situation. Most of all she was angry with herself.

Was it possible that within the space of one day she could have fallen in love? Surely not! Surely the appalling attraction Ryan had for her was just a physical thing? It had to be! Anything else would be unthinkable. Disastrous. For there could never be anything between them. Ryan's open contempt had made that clear. And yet that there was an attraction she could not deny. She had never dreamed that any man could make her feel so intensely female and vulnerable. That her body could ache with a gut-wrenching longing that was strong enough to make her forget the dictates of reason.

If Ryan's intentions had been to get Tracy into his bed, he had chosen the wrong moment to bring up her sister's name. That at least was something to be grateful for. And Tracy tried to push away the treacherous part of her, a part that was all raw sensation, which was not grateful at all. Balling a hand she hit it against the white-washed wall in a gesture of sheer frustration.

While she had struggled so hard to open the window she had forgotten the sensuous headiness of the hot scented air. She would never get any peace standing here, breathing it in. In any case it was time to go to bed. Tomorrow would be a long day. A hard day if she sensed Ryan's mood correctly. Best to be prepared for it.

She undressed quickly. Blessing the impulse that had led her to pack a travelling clock, she set the alarm for five-thirty, and put the clock on a chair which she pulled up beside the bed. No oversleeping tomorrow. Ryan would enjoy barging into the shack and hauling her out of bed—she would not give him that satisfaction.

But sleep did not come easily. Restlessly she tossed between the sheets, and tried everything from meditating to counting sheep and saying the alphabet backwards. Yet time and again a tall lean figure intruded upon her efforts, mocking her with a lift of cruel lips and pushing away the more mundane pictures she tried so hard to keep before her eyes. It was only towards morning that she finally fell into an exhausted sleep.

The shrilling of the alarm shocked Tracy into wakefulness. Lurching out a hand, she found the clock and pressed the knob. Then she fell back against the pillow. She was not *ready* to wake up. Her head throbbed and her eyes burned as for a while she lay quite still, vaguely wondering why the bed felt so strange and the mattress so uncomfortable.

She sat up with a start as the events of the previous day crowded in on her. How much time had passed since the alarm had woken her? Forcing open her eyes she saw that it was a quarter to six. God in heaven, in fifteen minutes there would be a thundering at her door and Ryan Demant would be standing there, demanding his pound of flesh.

For a moment she was tempted to roll over and go back to sleep. Let the arrogant Ryan make his demands, there was no way in which he could actually force her to comply with them. But apart from the fact that sleep had become impossible—she was suddenly very much awake—she knew that she was in no fit state to fight with Ryan. Nor did she want to, on this issue at least. She remembered thinking last night that it was important to prove to Ryan that he was wrong in his assessment of her. That she was tougher than he gave her credit for, that she did not resort to tricks to get out of a commitment. If respect was the only emotion she could exact from Ryan, that at least would be worth something.

She got out of bed, her toes curling on the cold stone floor, and made her way to the bathroom, which was as primitive as she'd thought. While she waited for the bath to fill, she cleaned her face, brushed her teeth, and combed her hair. Yesterday she had worn it loose, letting it fall to her shoulders. Today she tugged it back in a severe ponytail. It might not look as pretty, but it would not get in her way as she worked.

With only minutes to spare she was pulling the blanket over the bed. The knock at the door sounded just as she finished.

'Good morning.' He stood just beyond the doorway, as tall and as lithe as she'd remembered him. For Ryan it really was a good morning, Tracy thought grimly. He looked ruggedly virile in an open-necked shirt and tight denim jeans. His face had the freshness of one who had already spent some time out of doors.

'Good morning,' she returned flatly, wishing she felt as good as he looked.

'Sleep well?'

'Like a baby.'

'I wonder.'

Tracy made herself stand very still, outwardly indifferent as assessing eyes took in every detail of her appearance. As the slow gaze lifted from her figure back to her face she drew up her chin, summoning all her control so that she could meet his gaze squarely.

'I wonder,' he said again. A hand reached out so suddenly to touch her face that Tracy was unable to suppress an instinctive quiver. 'Babies don't wake up with pale cheeks.' The hand moved upwards, feather-light. 'Nor with dark bags beneath their eyes.'

Inside Tracy every nerve seemed to scream a protest. Sometime during the night she had resolved to withstand his seductiveness. And now it was starting again, sooner than she had expected, and already her treacherous senses were beginning to respond.

'My appearance should be of no concern to you,' she said stiffly.

He laughed softly. 'What concerns me is your mattress.'

'You'd like it to be the same as yours.' The words flashed out, almost without thought.

'We established that yesterday,' he agreed, and she saw his eyes linger, quite deliberately, on her lips. At the memory of how she had responded to his kisses less than twelve hours ago, her cheeks grew hot.

'But actually,' he went on, and now a sardonic note had crept into his tone, 'I was thinking of the mattress itself. It couldn't have been comfortable.' His eyes went beyond her, to the bed in the shack. 'I'd forgotten quite how rough it was.'

'You won't get me into your bed, Ryan.'

Something flickered in the dark eyes, so that Tracy found herself tensing. But when Ryan spoke again his voice was even. 'I was going to suggest that you use one of the guest rooms. You'd sleep better and be more able to face a day's work.'

So he had decided to put her in her place, had he? Tracy shot him one of her sweet smiles. 'Thank you, but I have no intention of moving.' A deliberate glance at her watch. 'Three minutes after six. Isn't it time you told me what to do?'

She had hoped to discomfort him, but a wicked grin told her she hadn't succeeded. 'In some ways your sister will never be the girl you are,' he observed. 'Come along, Tracy.'

She followed him, not certain whether she'd received a compliment. Ryan, it seemed, had a knack of making her feel uncertain. And that was not a comfortable state for someone who'd been reasonably confident and content with life until yesterday.

They got into a truck parked at the back of the farmstead. Ryan started the ignition and Tracy asked,

'Where are we going?'

'The orchards. Ever painted trees, Tracy?'

'On paper.'

'Now you'll paint them in the flesh so to speak.' He grinned at her. 'We paint the trunks to ward off disease.'

She'd seen the white barks yesterday, and there were white-painted trees where they drove now. Evidently the orchards extended a long way, and there were areas that had not been done yet. She wondered if the work would be back-breaking, whether Ryan would be demanding.

'I can do that,' she said lightly, giving him no hint of her thoughts.

His eyes left the road to look at her, but he made no comment.

A mile further along the road he drew the truck to a halt, reached beneath the seat, and brought out a thermos-flask and a cool-bag. 'Breakfast,' he announced. 'And this is a good place to have it.'

He opened his door, and Tracy opened hers and got out. It was indeed a lovely place for a picnic breakfast, she saw in a glance, as she walked a few steps away from the truck and looked around her. They must have been on one of the outer perimeters of Umhlowi, for there were fruit-trees only on one side of the road. A cliff-edge was on the other side, and without waiting for Ryan, Tracy left the road and walked a little way through the prickly, wind-swept scrub.

A bench stood near the edge, and Tracy stood beside it and looked out over the ocean. It was very early. In the eastern sky the sun was just beginning to lift from the horizon, but over the sea hung a grey haze that blurred the line between sea and sky, making them one great misty expanse. Later in the day it would be hot, unbearably hot perhaps, but now the air was fresh and invigorating, with the special salty smell that Tracy loved. This would be a beautiful spot in the daytime. She could picture herself sitting on the bench, looking out over the water, watching the gulls and the fishing-trawlers. She would be able to sit here for hours, just drinking in the utter peacefulness of the scene, wondering how she would capture it on film. And then she remembered that such an opportunity would never come her way. She would be at Umhlowi a month only, and if she judged Ryan correctly most of that time would be spent working.

'That's where we were yesterday.' The object of her thoughts was beside her, holding out an arm.

'Yes.'

The afternoon's sailing was still vivid in her mind. It had been so beautiful, that and the lovemaking that had followed it. Which had made Ryan's callousness at the end of it all the more of a shock.

In a brittle voice she said, 'You mentioned breakfast.'

'Of course.' There was a sudden hardness in his tone.

She watched him uncork the thermos and pour coffee into plastic mugs. He gestured to powdered milk and paper-wrapped sugar, and then he took a packet of rusks from the bag.

'Help yourself,' he invited brusquely.

Her mouth was dry with tension, and her throat felt sore. She wasn't a bit hungry, but she took a steaming mug and forced herself to reach for a rusk. There had been a time yesterday when things had gone so well between them, now there was a barrier that was as tangible as if it had been built of brick.

In the event she was glad of the hot drink, it was balm to the dry throat and mouth. Ryan dipped a rusk into his coffee, and after a moment Tracy did likewise. With a long day's work ahead of her it might be best if she ate. She took a bite of the dunked biscuit, normally hard as rock and found to her surprise that it was delicious.

She had a second cup of coffee, but when Ryan suggested another rusk she shook her head.

'It's going to be a long day,' he warned.

'I know,' she said politely.

He made a sudden impatient sound in his throat. 'Do you think you're achieving anything with this coolness?'

She shrugged, as if she didn't understand the question. 'I don't know what you mean. I'm merely complying with your terms. I'm taking Derrick's place for a month.'

'You know darn well what I'm talking about. Stop being so damned elusive.'

She glanced around her. They were so isolated, and he sounded so angry. She was a little frightened.

The movement of her eyes didn't escape him. If anything it seemed to make him angrier. Before she could move he had thrown down his cup, had seized her wrists and was pulling her against him. 'Do you think I'm going to throw you off the cliff? Is that what you think?'

She tried flippancy. 'Of course not. You need me to paint trees.'

His hands went to her shoulders, gripping them a moment before he shook her. It occurred to her that she might have driven him too far.

'Last night you weren't so damned cool,' he said between gritted teeth.

'That was last night.'

He was so close to her that she could sense every inch of the long, muscled body even though she was not in contact with it. She tilted her head back to look at him, and was immediately sorry for it as she was filled with sudden excitement. In his impatience and frustration there was something infinitely dangerous about Ryan. The aura he gave off was purely sexual, Tracy thought wildly. There was something devilishly attractive in the set of the lips, in the anger-sparked eyes, in the rugged cheekbones. There was nothing remotely lover-like in the way he held her, and yet her excitement was such that she could feel her heart thudding against her ribs, and she had to restrain an impulse to step closer to him. In his present mood the movement would inflame him, and he would make love to her. It would be a savage kind of lovemaking that would have nothing to do with affection, but would be purely physical. She would enjoy it, a part of her that she had never suspected existed until yesterday, would enjoy it. But later, when sanity had returned, as it must, she would regret it.

'Your sister may be a schemer but at least she doesn't play a come-go game with Derrick.' His voice was heavy with contempt. 'Perhaps she's more honest than you after all.'

The words hurt, as they were meant to. But Tracy knew she could not let him know it. Somehow retaining her outward show of coolness she said, 'Think what you like, Ryan. Isn't it time to get to work?'

They walked back to the truck in silence and didn't speak again until they reached the orchard where they were going to work. Ryan got out, and Tracy got out too, without waiting to see if he would come round to her side to open the door. She did not think his mood extended to small courtesies. In the back of the truck were great tins of paint and brushes, which he started to unload. There were also denim overalls, and he threw her a pair, curtly ordering, 'Put them on.'

Tracy would have liked to change out of her own clothes first. It would be hot, for already so early in the morning there was a mugginess in the air. But there was not even an outhouse where she could undress in private, and so she just slipped the overalls on over her jeans and shirt. They were several sizes too big for her, but she rolled them up at the ankles and the wrists.

She turned to Ryan and saw that he was watching her. For the moment the hardness was missing from his face. His eyes glimmered with amusement, but there was also something else in his expression—not quite a tenderness but a quality very like it. Tracy wondered if he saw the pulse that leaped suddenly in her throat.

'A bit big for me,' she said, stating the obvious but needing something to say.

'An understatement. A worklady in danger of drowning in her working gear.'

When he teased it was almost impossible to remain cool with him. She found herself smiling. 'Do you have anything smaller?'

'This was the smallest I could find. Have to buy you something in the village—if working overalls come in pint sizes.'

The amused exchange was just a respite, Tracy soon discovered. Ryan intended her to work, and there would be no letting up merely because it was hot, or because she was female, or because she was not used to manual labour. She wanted him to help her find Allison, and he would not do so unless she did Derrick's work first.

Which suited her down to the ground, she told herself firmly as she sloshed white paint around the bark of an orange tree. She wanted no favours from Ryan Demant. She would only have to pay for those she received and in any such transaction she would be the loser.

There was no conversation between them as they worked. It was very hot, and beneath the denims Tracy felt prickles of sticky heat all over her body.

Her eyes blurred from the white of the paint and the dazzle of the sun, and there was strain at her back and in her thighs and calves.

Now and then she glanced at Ryan. If he was hot and tired there was no sign of it. He worked so easily, despite her best endeavours he seemed to do three trees to every one that she managed. How many trees were there anyway at Umhlowi? Thousands, Tracy guessed, and she wondered why farmers as wealthy as Ryan and Derrick did not employ people to help them. Surely it was the way most men would operate. But Ryan did not fall under the category of 'most men', that much she had learned very quickly. As for Derrick, until she met him she could not pass judgment, but she sensed that Derrick was weaker than Ryan, and that he followed his older brother's dictates.

At length it was time to break for lunch. Tracy was so tired that her limbs were shaking. She found some shade and squatted there while Ryan went to the truck to fetch the food.

'Hungry?' he asked as he came back to her with a different flask and the cool-bag.

'Starving,' she admitted.

Her thirst was even greater than her hunger. She drank three cups of ice-cold water, and then began to make inroads on the sandwiches Ryan had brought. They were delicious, beef and lettuce and a smidgeon of mustard wedged between slices of fresh rye bread. But even if they had not been so good she'd have eaten; after the hours of labour her body cried out for nourishment.

'What are you thinking?' she heard Ryan ask.

She turned and saw that he had been watching her. 'That I'll never look at an orange with the same eyes again,' she told him feelingly.

He laughed, and even through her weariness she

thought how laughter transformed his face, relaxing it, warming his eyes. 'That bad was it? Perhaps if I had got your sister into the orchards I'd have scared her away from Derrick in a day.'

'You persist in thinking of Allison as a villain, don't you?'

'Just as a schemer.'

'Derrick the saint,' she said sarcastically.

'Derrick the boy who has fallen for every pretty girl who ever came his way,' his brother said lazily. 'No pretty girl has ever had to try very hard to rouse Derrick's interests. But this is the first time he's been crazy enough to contemplate marriage. Allison must have played the game better than most.'

No good defending Allison. She had tried it before with no success. She said instead, 'You've a low opinion of your brother.'

'On the contrary, I'm very fond of him. I happen to know his weaknesses.'

'You don't believe they love each other?'

'I'm prepared to concede a certain amount of infatuation on both sides.'

The words could only mean that he did not believe in love himself, *for* himself. The knowledge gave her no joy. Which was ridiculous in the extreme, for she had decided last night that her feelings for Ryan could only be physical—how could they be anything else after just one day?—and in the circumstances it shouldn't matter one way or another if he was incapable of love.

But it did matter.

'It's obvious that you've never been in love yourself,' she said, a little flatly.

'Is it?' There was something enigmatic in the eyes that swept her face.

Leave the subject alone, warned a sensible inner voice. But Tracy did not feel sensible. She was in a mood to challenge, to defy.

'Yet there must have been women in your life.'

His mouth lifted. 'There have been women. Several in fact. I'm thirty-four, Tracy, and no saint. I've taken my pleasures where I could find them. And most women, I've observed, have been happy to play along.'

'They've understood the rules of your game.'

'Of course.'

'A kiss today, goodbye tomorrow, and no strings attached.'

'Precisely.'

That was all a woman-man relationship meant to him. A game. A man like Ryan would have no trouble finding women with whom to enjoy himself. Women who were glamorous and sophisticated, who were content with the wining and dining and fine presents that any mistress of Ryan's could undoubtedly expect.

It would be so easy to drift into a relationship with him. Alone together for a month in the lovely seclusion of Umhlowi, what would be more natural? Or more tempting? Ryan Demant was the most attractive man she had ever met. A man to stir the blood and rouse the senses. She was aware of him every moment, whether she was painting trees or sharing a meal with him. And Ryan had made it clear that he would not be averse to having sex with her.

But sex was all it would ever be with him. Sex with a girl who was reasonably attractive and very accessible. A game to be enjoyed while it lasted; when it was over it would be forgotten in about as much time as it took for a rolling dice to be put back in its box.

But it was a game in which Tracy could never take part. It would tear her to shreds when it ended, for she would not be able to look on it as a game. Sex and love must go together as far as she was concerned. To fall in love with Ryan Demant would mean disaster. She would not let herself fall in love with him, she resolved fiercely. And even as she did so, she wondered whether the resolve was already too late.

CHAPTER FIVE

SHE stood up abruptly, brushing crumbs and grass from her jeans. 'Isn't it time to get back to work?'

'Do you always cut short your lunch breaks?' he asked, shooting her an amused look, almost as if he knew the thoughts that had passed through her head.

'Quite often,' she said flatly, refusing to give him the satisfaction of thinking she had cut this break short on purpose.

'A glutton for punishment.' He uncoiled himself from the ground. 'All right then, Tracy, I'm ready to go back if you are.'

After the rest her leg-muscles ached when she walked. If she felt so stiff after one morning, how would she feel tomorrow, after a night's sleep? Tracy wondered ruefully.

'Feeling okay?' Ryan asked once, his tone mild and solicitous.

She darted him a smile. 'Terrific.'

His concern did not fool her. He would like nothing better than a chance to prove that she was not up to fulfilling her commitment, and if she did not, he would not take her to Allison. Despite his contempt for her sister, Tracy had the feeling that Ryan didn't care either way whether Derrick married her or not. If he *had* cared, he would have found a way of stopping them without her own intervention.

It was a long afternoon. It became more and more of an effort for Tracy to keep her expression relaxed and her shoulders from drooping with fatigue. Now and then, when Ryan's head was turned away, she glanced at her watch. She did not know when they would stop working, she knew only that the time had never passed more slowly.

When Ryan announced that they had finished for the day it was hard not to breathe a sigh of relief.

'Tired?' he asked.

'No.' And then after a moment, she admitted, 'A little.'

'Think you'll be able to keep this up for a month?'

Tracy lifted her chin as she smiled. 'Of course.'

Dark eyes ran impassively over her, taking in the face that was a little pale beneath the day's sunburn, the small figure trembling with tiredness beneath the bulky man's overalls. 'Don't try too hard,' he cautioned.

'I'm fine, Ryan.'

'You'll feel it by tomorrow.'

She looked at him curiously. 'You've decided to let me off?'

'Of course not.' Ryan's grin was rakish. 'You'll fill in for Derrick, just as we agreed. I'm just telling you not to push yourself too hard at the beginning.' His expression changed again, and now the amusement was gone from his face. Softly he said, 'You've already proved that you're a spunky girl.'

There was nothing soul-stirring or romantic in the words, and yet Tracy felt happiness leaping suddenly inside her. However much she might tell herself that what Ryan thought of her did not matter, she knew it was not true. It mattered very much. Too much perhaps.

'Oh for a nice warm bath,' she sighed as they were driving back to the farmstead.

'You'd enjoy a swim even more.'

She turned to look at him. 'You're going to the beach?'

'I'm going to swim in the pool. You haven't seen it yet, Tracy?'

'I didn't even know that you had one.' Though she should have guessed. Umhlowi wouldn't lack much in the way of luxury.

It had been built in the midst of a small walled garden, and was so secluded that it was no wonder she had not known of its existence. The sides and bottom of the pool were blue-tiled, giving an inviting impression of coolness. Here and there on the lush green lawn which surrounded the pool there were trees, so that one could choose to lie in the sun or the shade according to one's fancy.

That Ryan should look dynamic in white swimming-trunks that clung to narrow hips while emphasising the muscularity of a superbly tanned and muscled torso was something Tracy knew already, but the sight still caused the breath to catch in her throat. What made his attraction all the more potent was that it was so effortless. His good looks were as natural a part of him as his aura of power and sexuality. That he must be aware of his attraction, that women must have been dazzled by him all his life, did not seem to detract from the basic fact.

Tracy sat at the side of the pool, paddling her feet as she watched him ready himself for a dive. For a long moment he was quite still, sleek and perfect as a marble statue, the long legs taut, the feet lifted at the heels, the arms stretched out before him. With the slightest of movements he levered himself away from the edge, and a moment later he had entered the pool with a dive that caused no more than a ripple on the surface of the water.

For half a minute at least the water was still until

yards further a dark head surfaced. Ryan began to swim, his arms moving in strokes that were rhythmic and powerful. Three lengths of the pool were quickly covered, and then he stopped near Tracy's feet and stood up.

'You're not coming in?'

'In a moment.'

His eyes sparkled as they grinned up at her, the lashes looking incredibly long. His teeth were very white against the wet tanned face. He took a step closer, and she saw the muscles ripple in the broad chest and shoulders.

'Come on.' He was laughing at her. 'Not scared are you?'

Only scared of you, she thought a little wildly. Scared of the effect you're having on me. I've never felt like this before, and I'm not sure how to cope with it.

'Just taking my time,' she grinned back at him.

'Not the only thing you take your time about.' The sparkle was still in his eyes, but his voice had changed. It was not hard to know what he meant. There had been sexual tension between them from the moment they'd met. Her heart was suddenly thudding very hard against her ribs. For a long moment his eyes held hers, and she wondered if he knew that breathing had become difficult.

And then suddenly, unexpectedly, she felt his fingers on the soles of her feet and she gasped.

'Ticklish are you?' he asked softly, as she tried to pull away from him, only to find her ankles held firmly.

'Ryan, don't!'

It was hard to retain her composure. She was ticklish, but only a bit. It was not the teasing that caused her the most discomfort but the sensuousness of the fingertips on her soft soles. Feather-light, they had found the most sensitive areas of her feet, and were sending sensations up her legs and along her spine that made her feel like doing anything but laugh.

'Don't,' she whispered on a dry throat.

The tickling stopped, though Ryan's hands still held her ankles. Tracy drew a breath of relief. She was about to pull away from him, when he tugged at her feet. Her hands flew back in an attempt to save herself. But in vain. A moment later she was in the water.

'Why did you do that?' she scolded as she surfaced.

He came to her and put his hands on her shoulders. 'Some girls need more persuading than others.'

She met the gaze of the dark eyes, but could hold it only a moment before she had to look away. With any other man she would have been ready with a quick come-back. But Ryan made her feel vulnerable, unsure of herself. She was too aware of the closeness of the near-naked body to hers. Far too aware of the sudden need that stirred in her own body.

With a quick movement she twisted out of his hands. Without looking at him she began to swim, length after length without stopping, giving him never a glance as he swam easily alongside her. She tried hard to shut from her mind every thought of him, to concentrate instead on the ebb of the water, on the coolness that was so refreshing after the long hot day.

After a while she grew tired, and she turned on her back and floated, her eyes closed, the sun hot on her wet skin. Bliss, sheerest bliss. She would swim here often, only she would wait till Ryan had left the pool.

A hand caught the back of her waist. 'Stay as you are,' Ryan said softly.

Her eyes flicked open, and she made to stand up, but Ryan moved faster than she did. In an instant he had reached downward, so that she could feel his hand beneath her hips and her buttocks, the arm extending all the way along her back, supporting her.

Rationally she knew that it was the buoyancy of the water that made her weightless and able to lie on his arm. But it was the strangest sensation, and an exciting one. She could feel every one of Ryan's fingers at the tops of her thighs, the bare smooth skin of a flat stomach against her waist, and a pulse, somewhere at the top of his arm, against her cheek as she turned to look at him. She felt fragile, and at the same time intensely feminine and alive. She knew what was coming, and she knew that she wanted it as much as he did.

The sun had caught his wet hair, and it clung to his head like polished jet. The skin was taut over rugged cheekbones, and his eyes, no longer amused, looked down at her, deep with an expression that made the blood pound in her veins.

'You're lovely,' he said huskily.

'Am I?' The look she sent him from beneath her lashes was entirely alien to her. But then nothing that had happened since she'd come to Umhlowi was within the orbit of her experience.

'You know you are.'

The first kiss was light, gentle, his tongue playing around her lips and the corners of her mouth, the very lightness kindling a desire in her for something more.

He lifted his head and looked down at her. 'That's how lovely you are.'

'Ryan . . .'

Kiss me again, she'd wanted to say, but she stopped after his name, unable to go on. A little helplessly she looked up at him, not knowing the picture she made. Her lips were slightly parted, and her eyes held a kind of plea, while on his arm her slender figure had the delicacy of a mermaid.

Ryan made a sound in his throat, and then his head came down and he was kissing her again. Not a gentle kiss this time. There was passion in his lips, possessiveness and hardness and a need to explore the sweetness of her mouth. With an equal need exploding inside her, her lips parted willingly, her tongue meeting his in a kind of fierce joy, and her arm went around his neck in the desire to be closer to him.

The arm that had been supporting her body dropped and her body dropped with it. For a moment she wondered why, but only a moment, for then he was drawing her against him, both arms welding her tightly to him.

As his kisses grew even more demanding, Tracy's body was filled with an excitement that was almost unbearable. Every inch of her body seemed to be in contact with him now, her bare thighs against his, her breasts pushed hard against his chest, her feet clinging to his legs because she was out of her depth, her softness moulding itself to his hard planes and angles. Around them the water swirled with their movements, making for a sensuousness that made her head spin and her senses melt, so that there was little she could have denied him.

He tore his mouth from hers and looked down at her. 'I want you,' he said thickly.

She looked back at him wordlessly, her throat so full that she was unable to speak. What was there to say anyway? Didn't he know that he had her already?

He began to kiss her again. Still holding her, he made his way to the steps of the pool and carried her out, his arm beneath her legs now, his mouth never breaking contact with hers. She felt so dizzy that she did not wonder where he was taking her. When he put her down on a chaise-longue and lowered himself beside her she was not even surprised.

His hands moved over her, sliding over her throat and her shoulders, brushing her breasts beneath the bikini, then shaping the curves of her waist and hips. When his lips began to follow the same path Tracy moved restlessly, her wet body trembling with a hunger that was difficult to control. She made no effort to resist as he drew the slim straps from her shoulders and then the bikini from her body. And then his hands were cupping her breasts while his lips moved in the hollow between them, and she gave a little moan of pleasure.

It was only when she felt his hands at her panties that a measure of sanity returned.

'Ryan, no . . .'

'I want you.'

She wanted him too. How she wanted him! But this was not the time, the place.

She looked around her a little desperately. 'Someone will see . . .'

'Nobody will see. The pool is private, Tracy. Trees all around. Besides, there's nobody here.'

He was gathering her to him now, and lowering himself on to her at the same time, and she knew she had to put a stop to it. God, what a time for sanity to return! If only she had been able to think clearly in the pool she would have put a stop to the lovemaking earlier.

'No, Ryan.' Her throat was tight as she pushed her hands between their two wet bodies.

'I don't believe this.' His voice had hardened as he looked down at her.

She didn't believe it either. She had behaved stupidly in the past, but the last half hour must take the prize for stupidity.

He looked furious. 'Why did you lead me on?'

'I couldn't seem to help myself.'

'And now you're backing out.' The hands on her breasts tightened, hurting her. 'Why, Tracy, why?'

She couldn't answer him, she was trying so hard to hold back the tears.

There was a spark of understanding in his eyes. 'Because you're a virgin?'

It was a way out. She nodded.

'I wouldn't hurt you,' he said very gently.

She knew that. Knew too that even if he did hurt her it would not be deliberate, that the hurt would be momentary and drowned in the greater joy of fulfilment. There *would* be joy and fulfilment because she loved him.

There! She had admitted it to herself. She loved him. And that was the reason she couldn't surrender to him now. For Ryan did not love her, for him the lovemaking was just a pastime, a way of enjoying himself with an available woman.

'I'll be gentle,' he promised.

She thought she would choke on the tears in her throat. 'I know,' she whispered. 'But I can't.'

'Tracy . . .'

'I'm not ready. I'm sorry.'

'You should have known you weren't ready when we started this.' His tone was tight with frustration. 'Didn't you understand what was happening? You're more of a tease than I realised.'

She didn't try to defend herself. There was no defence. Not without an explanation. And it was an explanation she could not give him.

He swung himself off the chaise-longue and stood looking down at her. His body had dried partially in the hot sun, but here and there the skin was still wet. He looked very tall as he towered above her, the damp skin glistening like bronze, the muscled limbs taut. She longed to reach out and touch him, and clenched her fingers tightly to her sides.

'There will come a day when you'll forget your modesty,' he said at last. 'There's passion in that lovely body, Tracy, I've seen it, felt it.' His eyes lingered blatantly on her breasts, on the nipples that had swelled in his fingers. Until that moment she had forgotten her nakedness. Her cheeks grew hot.

'Please stop.' She made a little gesture of help-lessness as her hands lifted to cover her breasts.

'You don't need to plead with me.' His lips curled in contempt. 'I'll stop. Not because it's what *you* want, but because your little virgin games bore me.'

He picked up his towel and slung it over his shoulder. 'Six o'clock tomorrow morning, Tracy. See that you're ready.'

She watched him go, and knew it was not a moment too soon. The tears were thick on her lashes, and she didn't know how much longer she could keep them back. Ryan had said nothing about supper, but she didn't care. She couldn't eat a thing if she tried.

With trembling fingers she put the bikini-top back on and fastened the clasp. The sun shone down hotly but Tracy felt cold. A brightly plumaged bird was perched on the branch of a scarlet hibiscus, its shrill cries almost obscene on the still air. As if, like Ryan, it was mocking her.

It didn't matter what Ryan thought of her, she tried to tell herself. Worse by far if he knew the truth. Cynic that he was, he would be amused that she had fallen in love with him. He'd mock her all the more, but only after he'd taken her to his bed. The terrible thing was that at this moment, hurting with an agony she had not experienced before, she half-wished he had done just that.

For her the lovemaking would have been a wonderful thing, precisely because that was what it would have been. An act of love. But for Ryan she would have been no more than another in a long procession of women. She wanted more than that. So much more. She knew that what she wanted was beyond her reach which was why she was glad she had stood firm.

The days passed, and in many ways they were good

days. There were times when just being with Ryan
was wonderful, for she had come to accept that she
was in love with him, and that there was little she
could do about it. Working side by side, sharing meals
with him, talking, and finding out quite how much
they had in common; all these activities were ones
Tracy enjoyed to the fullest. She was building a
treasury of memories to cherish long after she had left
Umhlowi. She would remember Ryan at sunset,
relaxing after a day's work, with a pipe in his mouth
and a glass of beer at his side. She would remember
the long strong body at work, attending the trees or at
the wheel of a tractor. She would remember his
toughness and his maleness, and a sexuality that was
coupled with humour, a potent combination indeed.

It would not be difficult to remember. Harder by
far would be to forget. Yet the time would come when
she would have to forget; her future life depended on
it unless she meant to live only on memories.

The day after the incident at the pool had been the
worst. She had dreaded facing him the next morning,
certain that he would refer to it. He had been so angry,
so contemptuous when he'd strode away from the
pool, leaving her on the chaise-longue naked and
shivering. She had been sure that he would bring up
the subject, that he'd taunt her with it, perhaps that he
would try to make love to her again. But he never said
a word, neither did he touch her.

Sometimes, however, she would find him watching
her, and a quiver would go through her. At times like
these she was at a loss to quite define the expression
she saw in his face. It was a speculative expression, as
if Ryan wondered about the girl who had invaded his
home. There would be a bleak hardness in his eyes,
which frightened Tracy just a little. And now and then
there would be a spark of something that might have
been tenderness, but it would be gone so quickly that

she would wonder if she had imagined it. It unsettled Tracy even more than the hardness, perhaps because it was so fleeting, so elusive, and so hard to understand or explain.

The days were long and the work was hard, and there were no concessions from Ryan. Not that she had expected them, he had made himself clear on that point from the start. The first days were the most strenuous. Tracy's hands developed blisters and her muscles screamed in protest each time she used them, especially in the early mornings when she got stiffly out of bed. But she never told Ryan how she felt. The sight of him watching her was the spur that straightened her shoulders and brought a cheerful smile to her face, no matter how tired she felt. If he was waiting for her to beg for mercy he would wait a long time, she had resolved wryly, after he'd left her at the pool. She would do Derrick's work even if it killed her.

That this was in no danger of happening occurred to her when she'd been at Umhlowi a week. It was late one afternoon when Ryan called a halt to the day's work, and she realised that she could have gone on quite easily. I enjoyed myself today! The words hit her as she looked across at the tall figure making his way to the truck, and on a wave of exhilaration she wondered what his reaction would be if she said the words aloud.

Back in the shack she stripped off her clothes and looked in the mirror. Really looked. And was amazed at what she saw. She hadn't realised quite how much the last days had changed her. The mirror showed a body that was taut and healthy-looking. Her eyes were clear and sparkling against her tanned face, and here and there were streaks of pure gold where her hair had been touched by the sun. She looked good. She *felt* good. 'This life is agreeing with me,' she said aloud, and laughed at herself in the mirror.

After the disastrous afternoon at the pool she had not swum there again. Instead it had become habit to shower instead. She would soap herself with water from the basin before turning on the taps of the shower. Ancient and creaky it was, with tepid water spurting out in erratic fits and starts, so that she never spent as much time beneath it as she'd have liked.

Feeling good about herself today, she worked up a great foaming lather of soap and spread it all over her body. She went to the shower and turned on the taps. Nothing happened. She turned them further. No water came out. Disbelievingly she stared at the taps, then gave the wall a kick, thinking perhaps that might help. Still nothing.

Thoroughly frustrated she went back to the basin. She was so full of soap that it would take ages to get it all off by hand, but she had no alternative.

No water emerged from the taps of the basin. She turned them all the way, she pushed, she pulled them. In vain. This wasn't happening, she thought in dismay. There'd been water every day, there'd been water five minutes earlier, a trickle admittedly, but water all the same. What had happened to it now?

On soapy bare feet she padded back into the bedroom and looked at herself in the ancient mirror. Lather from head to foot. And no way of getting it off. Except one. And that was not a way she would consider.

She would *not* go to the farmhouse. *Could not!* Covered in soap and without a stitch of clothing! No way was she going to show herself to Ryan in this state.

There had to be *some* way of getting off the soap. But there was none. She had to admit it to herself at last. She had to go to the house, had to ask Ryan to let her use his shower. What made it even more humiliating was the fact that she could put on no clothes over the lather. And the only towels she possessed left much to be desired in the way of size. She took the biggest one and wrapped it round her, wishing that it covered more of her.

Ryan was sitting on the verandah, sipping his beer. As Tracy came up the steps his eyes were wide with delighted disbelief.

'What on earth . . .?' he began.

'I need to use your shower,' she said stiffly. 'If you have water that is.'

He stared at her a moment longer, before saying cheerfully, 'Gallons of it. Like to tell me why you need it?'

'I have a feeling you should be telling me,' she said ruefully. 'There's not a drop of water in the pipes, Ryan.'

'I should have warned you.'

If it was meant to be an apology it didn't sound like one. His lips were tilted at the corners, and his eyes were bright with mischief.

'Warned me of what?' Tracy demanded. 'Do you realise this is the most ridiculous situation I've ever been in?'

'And probably the funniest.' He laughed suddenly, the sound of it so warm and amused that Tracy was hard put to stand on her dignity and stop herself from laughing too. Somehow she managed. Ryan owed her water and an explanation, she was not sure which should come first.

'I'm not laughing *at* you,' he said at last softly. 'Surely you realise that, Tracy my dearest?'

No matter that the endearment meant nothing to him, it gave her a moment of intense pleasure, but now was not the moment to savour it.

'The water?' she prompted.

'Rain-water. Remember I told you about the tank that feeds the shack? It must have run dry.'

And she had never thought of checking the water-level. Later, when she could think rationally, she would know that Ryan could have checked it himself; that perhaps he had hoped she would come begging for the use of a bathroom, though he could not have envisioned the exact circumstances in which she would do it.

Now she could only look at him. 'I'm going to the bathroom.'

He came to her. 'I'll take you there myself.'

It was a moment before she understood that he intended to carry her. 'You'll get your clothes full of soap.'

'It will be worth it.'

He scooped her up in his arms and carried her into the house. She knew she should protest, but she also knew that she loved him, and that she did not have the strength to open her lips and tell him to put her down. Instead, this was one more memory she would cherish.

His shoulder was hard against her head, and she could feel the thud of his heart, and a peculiarly male smell filled her nostrils. Last time he had carried her had been from the pool, and he had been kissing her. It had been exciting, no matter the disaster that had followed. This, in its way, was just as exciting.

He took her to his own bathroom. Only then did he put her down. With the scanty towel wrapped around her, she watched as he turned on the taps. The water was spurting from the shower when he said, 'Ready?'

'You can leave me now.'

As he turned to her, the look of devilry in the dark eyes made her catch her breath. 'Not a chance, you know that.'

She must have known it, albeit subconsciously, while he had been carrying her.

She moistened her lips. 'You can't expect me to shower while you watch.'

'You know what I expect,' he said softly. His eyes

met hers, and adrenalin went pumping suddenly and swiftly through her system.

He came to her, and his hand was on the towel, he wanted to take it from her but she kept hold of it. It was no more than token resistance on her part, but some resistance seemed necessary.

'I don't need you to rinse the soap off me,' she said through the thudding in her ears.

'And you know I'm going to do it all the same. Don't fight me, Tracy.' His voice was husky.

She loved him so much, mind and body ached for him. In the circumstances her resistance was low. He gave a little tug and the towel fell away.

He stood looking at her, his gaze sweeping her body, and then his eyes came up, and the expression she saw in them made her legs feel suddenly weak. 'I must look a sight,' she said, to break the silence between them.

'Quite a sight indeed.' He was so close to her that she not only heard his laughter, she could almost feel it shaking his chest.

'A sight I'll never forget,' he said, and then he was propelling her beneath the shower, following her into it, fully clothed.

CHAPTER SIX

IN moments they were both wet. Ryan insisted on rinsing off the soap, and Tracy let him. She had reached the stage where there was little she could have denied him. But there was more to it than that—his hands sliding over her soapy body gave her a sensuous pleasure that she wouldn't have wanted to miss. I'm shameless, she thought, and I don't even care any more.

Water was streaming from their hair, Ryan's clothes

were soaked. Denims and shirt clung to his body, moulding his legs, his arms, his chest. He was laughing again, his teeth white against his tan, his eyes sparkling, his hair wild. He had never looked more sexual, more attractive.

'You're wet through,' she shouted to him through the water.

'Don't I know it!'

'You're crazy, Ryan!'

His hands went to her shoulders, sliding down over her arms. 'We're both crazy.' He caught her wrists in his fingers, bringing her closer to him. 'Perhaps that's why we belong together, Tracy.'

Excitement was a wild thing inside her. He was speaking in a way he had never spoken before. We belong together. On the verandah he'd called her his dearest. If only his interpretation of belonging was the same as hers. But it wasn't, even through her excitement she knew that.

Water streamed over their heads as he kissed her. A searching kiss that seared her senses and forced a response from her. She moved against him blindly, her hands gripping his shoulders, her thighs up hard against his, driven by the need to be as close to him as she could be, to let herself love him. The water flowed unheeded. There was only the wild thudding of their hearts and a mutual, passionate exploration of lips and tongues. This was how it had been in her dreams at night, only this was more wonderful. Certainly crazier. As one long drugging kiss merged into another she knew how much she had been wanting him in the days since they'd quarrelled.

When he stepped away from her and out of the shower she looked at him without comprehension. Was he rejecting her? Disappointment stabbed inside her. He couldn't be rejecting her, not now, not at this moment.

She moved away from the stream of water, and heard him say, 'Stay where where you are.'

'Ryan . . .'

'Yes.' He was tearing at the buttons of his sodden shirt. 'I'm taking off my clothes. We don't need any barriers between us, Tracy.'

He was beautiful, she thought, as he came back to her. The most beautiful man in all the world. The only man she wanted, would ever want.

With surprising tenderness he brought her into the circle of his arms. For a long moment they stood looking at each other, their only physical contact the loose clasp of his arms around her body, her hands on his shoulders. Tracy's mouth was dry, and her heart was beating so hard that she was sure he must hear it above the whoosh of the shower.

And then they closed the gap that separated them. He did not have to draw her to him, it was a mutual coming-together. Tracy ached to be near him, and the hardness of his body was evidence that he wanted her too. A sigh of pleasure shuddered through her as he began to kiss her throat and her shoulders, and then moved down to her breasts, where his lips teased each nipple in turn. His hands moved over her, sliding to her waist, to her hips, pulling them closer against him, and all the while his lips played on her body. And she was kissing him too, letting her own lips explore the hard planes of his shoulders while her hands learned the shape of his chest and his back, hearing him groan when she touched a sensitive area. She had never made love to a man, had never particularly wanted to, but instinct told her what to do now.

The last remnants of sanity were fleeing fast, but she knew what was coming. And she knew that this time there could be no holding back. Not that she had any wish left to hold back.

She wanted to given him pleasure, just as he was

giving her pleasure. Besides, she loved him, and for the first time she knew the true meaning of the need for fulfilment. He was going to take her to his bed, and she would go with him willingly. Last time she had resisted, not wanting to be one in a procession of females. Now even that thought no longer seemed to matter. She loved him, and she wanted him to make love to her. And if there were other women in his life, they were not here with him at this moment, beneath the streaming water. This was the only moment that mattered, not the ones that were in the past or those still in the future.

Their lovemaking had never been more erotic, nor more tender. I'm shameless, she thought, as she responded to him with an ardour beyond anything she had dreamed she was capable of. And I don't care. This is right and beautiful, and I'll enjoy what happens tonight and I'll never regret it.

He drew away from her with a sudden shuddering groan. 'You're so lovely.'

'You're lovely too.' She traced the outline of a shoulder very lightly with one finger.

'I want you to marry me.'

She gasped, her head jerking up, her eyes meeting his, unable to take in what she was hearing.

'Soon,' he insisted.

'Ryan—why?' Happiness was a crazy thing exploding inside her. But there was also confusion.

'Isn't it obvious?' he demanded huskily.

There was only one obvious reason for marriage, and that was love. She had loved him for days. Perhaps from the first moment she had met him, she thought now. But never once had he given her any indication that her feelings were reciprocated.

She was about to put her thoughts into words when he said, 'I want you in my bed, Tracy darling.'

He'd said *that* before.

'Have you any idea what you do to me?'

The hard body had told her already. A little shyly, she said, 'Yes.'

'I'm a normal man, Tracy, I can't go on like this. I want you, darling.'

She stretched out her arms to him. 'You have me,' she whispered.

He drew her against him a moment, and incredibly she felt a shuddering run through the taut male figure. Then he was putting her a little away from him.

'Not like this. You're not ready for it.'

'I am ready.' Love and desire had turned a self-sufficient girl into a passionate woman whom she didn't recognise. 'Make love to me, Ryan.'

'Witch!' His tone was amused, but his expression showed only longing and a kind of torment. 'A few days ago I'd have accepted the offer without a moment's hesitation.'

'You still can,' she whispered.

'No. It's marriage for you. It always has been.' He stepped away from her. 'I'm going to get dressed, and so are you, otherwise I won't be able to answer for my actions.' He looked down at her. '*Will* you marry me, Tracy?'

Her heart was in her eyes so that there should be no need of an answer. He hadn't said a word about love, she knew that. He desired her, and he wanted to know that she would be there for him whenever he wanted her. Once that would not have been enough for her. But she had never dreamed that she would love a man as much as she now loved Ryan. With time, perhaps he would come to love her. In the meanwhile, she loved enough for them both.

'Yes!' She smiled suddenly, radiantly. 'Of course I'll marry you.'

*   *   *

'What a wonderful surprise.' The delight in Marie Demant's eyes equalled the warmth of her words. 'Ryan, this is wonderful. Tracy, you must tell me all about it.'

All? Tracy glanced at Ryan, saw the sparkle in his eyes, and looked away quickly lest he try to make her laugh. There was no way she could tell his grandmother all that had happened. Mrs Demant would be shocked. Tracy barely believed it herself yet.

'Come and sit down, dear.' Mrs Demant gestured to the seat beside her. 'Where did you meet? How long have you known each other?'

Tracy looked up at the handsome man who was to be her husband. 'We've known each other about a week.'

'When is the wedding?' put in Patsy, Ryan's sister, a girl of about nineteen.

'We haven't set a date.' Tracy shook her head happily. 'We've been painting trees till today. My head's spinning, we haven't even begun to think of wedding-plans yet.'

'I thought Saturday would be a good day,' Ryan said smoothly.

'Painting trees?' asked his grandmother.

'Will Saturday suit you, Tracy?' Ryan asked.

'Painting trees?' The question was repeated. 'Seems to me you have some explaining to do, Ryan.'

Tracy looked from one to the other, the dynamic man, the frail woman, so seemingly different from each other in every way, and yet sharing the same brown eyes, and, she guessed, the same strength of character. For all her frailness Marie Demant had the look of a woman who demanded answers to questions, and received them. Perhaps she was the only person to whom Ryan deferred.

Tracy looked around her. The living-room where they were sitting was exquisite, furnished with antique furniture and persian carpets and a few lovely oil-paintings. A perfect back-drop for the aristocratic Mrs Demant. Had Ryan lived here too at one time? For the first time Tracy realised how little she knew about the man she was going to marry. Not that she minded. There would be time to learn, time to discover each other. A shared life of time.

'About those trees,' prompted Mrs Demant.

'We spent a few days painting trunks,' Ryan said laconically.

'Why?' This from Patsy.

Tracy was confused. All this talk of trees. Ryan's family must know the ins and outs of farming almost as well as he did. She'd have thought they would be more interested in the topic of the wedding. Only minutes ago Ryan's grandmother had sounded delighted with the news.

'They get painted to prevent disease,' Tracy explained.

'I know that,' Mrs Demant said quietly. 'My question is—why you, Tracy? Well, Ryan?'

'I was working in Derrick's place,' Tracy said quickly, before he could speak.

'Derrick's place?'

'That was the bargain. That we'd go after Derrick and Allison before Allison's birthday.' She looked from one amazed face to another. 'Allison is my sister.'

'Allison Galland!' Patsy exclaimed. 'I knew your name was familiar. Why didn't I make the connection?'

'What I'm wondering is,' said Mrs Demant very quietly, 'why it was necessary for Tracy to work in Derrick's place.'

'I thought I'd explained.' Tracy was beginning to feel agitated.

'*You* did. My grandson has not. I know that look of yours, Ryan. I demand to know why this young woman, the future mistress of Umhlowi at that, was expected to paint trees.'

'But . . .'

Ryan cut Tracy short. 'My grandmother means,' he explained grinning, 'that with a full staff of farm-workers she sees no reason for you to have worked in the orchards.'

'Right,' said his grandmother.

'Wrong,' responded Ryan crisply, without a hint of remorse. 'Only minutes ago, Grandma, you were delighted at the news of our wedding. You might as well know that if I hadn't—persuaded—Tracy to stay at Umhlowi, and work with me ten hours a day in the orchards, there would be no wedding.'

Patsy gave a shout of laughter. 'You conned her!'

'It was the only way I could think of getting her to stay any length of time.'

'You're a reprobate, Ryan,' said Marie Demant but her eyes were twinkling. 'Of course I do see that you had to keep this lovely young woman around long enough for her to get to like you.'

'I knew you'd understand,' he agreed, and Tracy, head whirling with this new set of amazing facts, thought he had never looked quite so handsome.

'So you do have farmworkers,' she said.

'Quite a few. And they're all blessing you for an extra week of leave. As is Letitia.'

'You sent Letitia away too?' Now Mrs Demant looked taken aback.

'Who is Letitia?' Tracy wanted to know.

'The housekeeper.'

'I thought a woman comes in from the village. . . .' Tracy stopped, understanding that she was being naive.

'So you were alone together,' Mrs Demant said.

'You've shocked Grandma,' Patsy giggled. 'Grandma, darling, these are the eighties.'

'As it happens,' Ryan told them, 'Tracy slept in the shack.'

'That dreadful old place!' his grandmother exclaimed. 'Ryan, I don't believe this! What have you done to the poor girl? Making her slave in the orchards from dawn to dusk. Having her sleep in the shack. Did you sleep on the floor, Tracy?'

'There was a bed.'

'But with an awful mattress, if I remember rightly. I thought it was thrown out long ago. And the plumbing was antiquated to say the least.'

Tracy's eyes met Ryan's. He was watching her, laughing at her, no, not *at* her but *with her*. A private joke that would give them amusement often in the future.

For a moment it was as if nobody else was in the room with them. The memory of the lovemaking under the shower was still vivid. A warm glow spread through Tracy's body, and she knew that if they were alone together now they would be making love once again. And this time there would be no stopping.

But they were not alone. On the periphery of her vision she saw Mrs Demant and Patsy watching her a little curiously.

She smiled at them both. 'I was so tired that I didn't mind the mattress, and the plumbing wasn't too bad.'

'As a matter of fact the plumbing behaved beautifully,' Ryan said, and there was a gleam in his eye.

Quickly, because she didn't trust him when devilry took him, Tracy said, 'It really wasn't that bad.'

'Well you deserve a lot better. You'll be staying here at Sea View with Patsy and me until the wedding. I still haven't had an answer on the date.'

'As soon as we can make it.'

The look in Ryan's eyes sent new warmth flooding

through Tracy. To her his expression was blatant. I want to make love to you, it seemed to say, I want you in my bed. She wondered if Mrs Demant and Patsy had caught the expression and understood it.

'You're in a hurry for a confirmed bachelor of thirty-four years,' Patsy declared.

'Tracy and I are going after Derrick and Allison. If we're going to be travelling companions I want us to be married first.'

The glance his grandmother sent him was searching. For a woman who had been reared in a less liberal age she was shrewd, Tracy realised. Mrs Demant knew her grandson well, knew that travelling with a woman without being married to her had not deterred him in the past, must be questioning why this time was different. If only their marriage could be founded on a stronger foundation than the fact that Ryan desired physical intimacy, she wished now. She felt a pang of depression which she swiftly cast aside. Love would come in due time, she had to believe that. In the meanwhile she would enjoy whatever Ryan had to give.

She was relieved when Mrs Demant called a pause to her questions, and asked Ryan to fetch a bottle of champagne from the wine cellar. This was an event to be celebrated, she declared with a warmth that endeared her to Tracy. The champagne would chill a while, and they would have it with their dinner.

She turned to Tracy. 'Have you spoken to your mother?'

'Not yet. I'd like to phone her if I may.'

'Of course, my dear, you must phone. Use the one in the study. Please tell her that we would like her to come down just as soon as she can make it, and that we look forward to having her as our guest.'

This was the family from which Tracy had been

sent to rescue Allison. Tracy wondered whether her mother would revise her views when she met them.

'You're marrying a Demant?' Lucille Galland was flabbergasted. 'The young man Allison went off with?'

'His brother Ryan. Mom, I want you to come here for the wedding . . .'

'I don't understand! You've been away a week. I've been so worried.'

'I should have phoned you earlier.' Tracy was instantly remorseful. Apart from a phone-call made in the village before catching the taxi to Umhlowi, she had not spoken to her mother. She should have known she would be concerned. Was this what love did to one?

'How could you let yourself be caught too? You've always been the sensible one. There's something wrong about this family.'

'No, Mom, no. They're wonderful. Wait till you meet them.'

'At least . . . don't hurry things. Don't let them get out of control.'

Things have been out of my control almost from the moment I arrived here. I don't think I have the power to slow them down. I *don't want* them to slow down.

'I'm getting married on Saturday,' she said gently.

'Are you sure you know what you're doing?'

'Yes, Mom,' Tracy said firmly. 'I'm very sure.'

'In that case . . . Darling, you know I wish you every happiness.' Her mother's voice was husky, as if she was close to tears.

There was a lump in Tracy's throat as she said, 'And you'll come?'

'Try keeping me away. Call Allie to the phone.'

The hand that held the receiver was suddenly tight. 'Allison isn't here.'

'You *have* found her?' There was immediate concern in the voice at the other end of the line.

'Not exactly . . .'

'Tracy!'

'I know where she is. At least, Ryan knows where they are.'

'My God, Tracy, you let the one brother sweep you off your feet when you should have been stopping the other brother running away with Allison. I can't believe it!'

A movement caught Tracy's eye and she looked up. Ryan had come into the study. He was standing in the doorway, leaning against the jamb, one long leg crossed over the other, his hands pushed into his pockets. His eyes were lit with understanding. He lifted an eyebrow at her and she shook her head at him.

She took a breath. 'Allison isn't married yet. She won't be for a while, and we'll get to her in time. Mom, please don't worry. I'll explain it all to you when I see you.'

'Tracy . . .'

'Nothing is as you imagined it. You'll understand when you get here, really you will.'

They spoke a few minutes longer. Lucille Galland would have to arrange a few days' leave from the boutique which she managed. As the mother of the bride there were clothes to think about. Travelling arrangements to consider. She would phone Tracy when all her plans were in hand, would let her know exactly when to expect her.

'Difficult call?' Ryan asked sympathetically when Tracy put down the receiver.

'Not the easiest.'

He put his arm around her shoulder, and she let herself relax against the angular body. Ryan might not be in love with her, nevertheless he was the one person in whom she could safely put all her trust; with whom she would be able to share her joys and sorrows, just as she hoped that he would share his with her. In such a partnership it was not inconceivable that the feelings of affection and desire which he felt for her now would eventually turn to love in time.

'We Demants seem to have created havoc in the breasts of the Galland family,' he said.

She smiled up at him. 'Havoc aplenty.' And she knew that she would have it no other way, at least not as far as Ryan was concerned. Derrick was another matter. She still had to make up her mind about Ryan's brother.

But this was not the time to think about Derrick. Dinner was ready. They ate in the dining-room of Sea View, a beautiful room with walnut furniture and dull gold curtains and carpet. Candles in a graceful antique copper candelabrum gave the table an especially festive air. Looking at Mrs Demant and at Patsy, both dressed in clothes that were simple yet expensive, Tracy felt suddenly out of place.

'I brought so little with me,' she explained awkwardly. 'Just jeans and tops and this sundress. I didn't anticipate being away from home more than a day or two.'

'You look lovely just as you are.' Marie Demant spoke with the unaffected graciousness that seemed a natural part of her.

'Tracy will be buying herself a whole new wardrobe in the next few days,' said her husband-to-be.

'I have clothes at home,' she protested.

'You may need a few more,' Mrs Demant said tactfully.

'Mistress of Umhlowi and all that jazz,' Patsy put in with an irrepressible grin, apparently unawed by her grandmother's look of reproach.

Mistress of Umhlowi. The words had an odd ring to them. One she didn't associate with herself at all. Not that she minded. She was being made more welcome by the Demant family than she could have imagined.

The meal was delicious. Veal in a delicately flavoured sauce was served with tiny new potatoes and asparagus spears. Ryan opened the champagne, and as the cork exploded out of the bottle Patsy shouted, 'Hurrah!' Ryan poured the wine, and Marie Demant lifted a fine crystal glass in her fingers, waited for the others to lift theirs, and then she said, 'To Tracy and Ryan. Welcome to our family, Tracy, and may you both be very happy together.'

Tracy felt the heaviness of unexpected tears gathering in her eyes. Involuntarily she looked across at Ryan and saw him watching her. He could not know how much the simple toast had affected her, for he did not know that she loved him. He wanted her in his bed, and he saw marriage as his only way of getting her there. How amazed he would be to know that she had fallen in love with him. But she would not tell him. Not yet anyway. Instinct told her that Ryan was content with the way things were. Let him know that she loved him and he might feel restricted.

To hide her emotion she bent her head and began to eat. Patsy was laughing as she told a joke, and Ryan laughed with her, and by the time the joke had been told Tracy felt that she had herself under control.

Patsy had a fund of anecdotes, and the champagne had loosened both her tongue and her inhibitions. There was a merry atmosphere at the table. Mrs Demant might have intended talking about the wedding, but Patsy was not to be stopped, and as one joke merged into the next even Ryan's grandmother had to wipe the tears of mirth from her eyes.

'You've had enough to drink, sister mine,' Ryan said once.

'My pompous brother. Heavy-handed isn't he, Tracy, you'll have to learn to keep him in check.' Patsy giggled as she held out her glass for more champagne. 'Oh come on, Ryan, give me a little, you only get married once after all.'

Ryan gave in good-naturedly, and Patsy sipped with enjoyment. 'Grandma, aren't you amazed that Ryan's the first one to marry?' she said then. 'Derrick's always been the one with the eye for girls. You've met my younger brother, Tracy?'

'Not yet.'

'Oh, he's fun, you'll like him. But he's a real Casanova. I've lost count of Derrick's girls. I bet he's lost count too.'

'Patsy, I don't think Tracy wants to ...' Ryan began, but there was no stopping his sister.

'Only the prettiest girls for Derrick,' she rambled on. 'Perfect figures, perfect faces. Your sister must be a real doll.'

'Allison is pretty,' Tracy acknowledged, a light smile hiding her alarm. She had come to Umhlowi with a purpose in mind. Meeting Ryan, falling crazily in love with him, had clouded that purpose. The phone-call with her mother had made her a little impatient, as if her mother was being unnecessarily protective of a girl who was very nearly the legal age for marriage. Patsy's words brought back reality. Tipsy the girl might be, but she undoubtedly knew what she was saying. Tracy knew that the need to find Allison before she committed herself irrevocably to Derrick was as great as ever.

A hand reached across the table and closed on one of hers. She looked up and met Ryan's eyes. His hand was as comforting as the arm around her shoulder had been after the phone-call. Suddenly she felt better. Ryan knew the thoughts that passed through her head. Recognised her anxiety. And she knew that with Ryan to help her she had nothing to worry about after all.

Dessert was the perfect ending to the meal, a confection made with Grand Marnier and ice-cream. When it had been eaten, Mrs Demant led the way back to the living-room.

Coffee was served in lovely porcelain cups, so delicate that Tracy thought a careless flick of the finger might break them. Patsy had grown quieter, and the conversation went back to the wedding. Mrs Demant was eager to start planning the affair immediately.

'I don't think either of us wants a fuss,' Ryan said. And then, turning to Tracy, 'Or am I being too high-handed? I never thought of asking you, do you really want all the trimmings that go with a big wedding?'

I only want you. I want to be your wife. I want to love you, and share my life with you, and bear your children.

She shook her head. 'No.'

'A certain amount will be expected,' said Marie Demant. 'Ryan, you farm Umhlowi. It's the biggest estate in the area, certainly the most respected.'

There it was again. Status, position. Wealth, and both the responsibilities and the privileges that accompanied it. Tracy felt a small shiver of nervousness as she wondered what she was getting herself into.

'Let's compromise on a reasonably smart wedding,' Ryan smiled at his grandmother, and Tracy was touched at the warmth that flowed between them.

'There's no time for more than a compromise if you insist on rushing things,' Mrs Demant reproached.

'I do insist,' Ryan said firmly, with a look at Tracy that sent the adrenalin pumping rapidly through her system.

He got to his feet. 'Can I get anybody a liqueur?'

'Yes,' Patsy said with alacrity.

'I think not,' interposed her grandmother. 'You've had more than enough to drink already, child, and it's gone to your head because you're not used to it.'

'I'm not a child. We're celebrating. I'll have a liqueur please, Ryan.'

'If we're celebrating, I'll have one too.'

All heads turned at the sound of a new voice. A woman had entered the room. A very beautiful woman, tall and voluptuous, dressed in a silky wine-red trouser-suit which clung sexily to every voluptuous inch of her. Her hair was dark and glossy and swept away from her face in a chignon which enhanced the perfection of her classical features, and in her earlobes were diamonds. She was the very epitome of elegance and sophistication.

Tracy was even more conscious of her simple sundress. She was also, quite unaccountably, ill at ease.

'Why, Freda. Do come in, how nice to see you,' Mrs Demant said.

'I'm in already. As virtually one of the family I knew I'm always assured of a welcome.' Her voice was husky and she had a vivacious smile. 'How are you Marie? Patsy? Ryan, darling, you're looking virile as always. I haven't seen you for a few days.'

'I've been busy,' he said.

'So I hear,' Freda said.

'What will you drink, Freda?' Marie Demant asked.

'I leave the choice to Ryan. He always knows exactly how to please me.' Freda glanced at Ryan. 'So you're engaged to be married, darling?'

'Yes.' His face was devoid of expression.

'How did you know?' Mrs Demant asked. 'We only heard the news tonight ourselves.' She was as gracious as before but Tracy thought she detected a kind of tautness in her bearing. Was it her own tension that was making her imagine things? she wondered.

Freda shrugged. 'News travels quickly in the village. You know that my gardener and your housekeeper are friends.'

'I see.' Mrs Demant gestured towards Tracy. 'Freda, I'd like you to meet Miss Tracy Galland. Tracy is Ryan's fiancée. Tracy, this is Mrs Freda Antonis.'

A cool hand shook Tracy's briefly. 'Congratulations, Miss Galland.' Freda looked Tracy up and down a moment before saying. 'Charming, perfectly charming.'

If a response was called for, Tracy did not know what it should be. Feeling tongue-tied and inadequate she looked at the other woman. Charming, Freda had called her, but the word had a mocking sound. The expression in the beautifully made-up eyes told Tracy that the other woman considered her simple and unsophisticated and totally un-charming.

Patsy hiccuped suddenly. 'I think Freda is jealous.'

'How can I be when I've nothing to be jealous about?' Freda gave a husky laugh. 'And to prove it I shall congratulate the lucky bridegroom.'

Tracy watched her walk across the room to where Ryan was busy with the drinks. No, she thought, 'walked' was not the right word. Freda's manner of progression was a swaying of hips and thighs which was so totally sensuous that it needed a different word to describe it.

'Darling, congratulations.'

She moved up against him and her hands reached up to cup his head. And then she was kissing him, a kiss on the mouth that must have lasted a full ten seconds.

The silence in the room lasted just as long. Even Patsy was moved to muteness. Tracy's heart was thudding so loudly that she was sure it could be heard by everyone.

The kiss ended. As if nothing out of the ordinary had occurred, Freda took a glass from the drinks table, and turned back into the room with that same vivacious smile.

She looked at Mrs Demant. 'This must be a happy occasion for you, Marie.'

Tracy was feeling more and more uncomfortable. If she could have left the room inconspicuously she'd have done so. There were undercurrents here, and the fact that she did not understand them made them all the more unpleasant.

Ryan said quietly, 'It's a happy occasion for me too.'

Both Freda and his grandmother swung round to look at him. In the moment before Freda turned her head Tracy caught the expression in her eyes— 'poison' was the word that came to mind.

But her voice was pure honey. 'And I'm happy for all of you.' She turned back to Tracy. 'You're a lucky girl, Tracy. Clever too.' She smiled brightly. 'You must tell us all how you caught this confirmed bachelor.'

'There's nothing *to* tell.'

'Oh but how boring.' Freda pouted. 'We're all dying to hear.'

The arm around Tracy's shoulders came unexpectedly. She hadn't seen Ryan come to her from across the room. 'She doesn't have to tell anyone a thing,' he said easily. 'Some secrets are only meant for two.'

Languidly Freda glanced at her watch. 'Well, I must go. I have an appointment and I just stopped by here first to offer my contratulations.'

She walked to the door, a sensuous, elegant, confident figure. Only Patsy's tipsy giggle marred her exit.

CHAPTER SEVEN

WITH Freda's departure the atmosphere in the room lost its strain. For a while they talked about the arrangements for the wedding. Marie Demant was concerned about seating arrangements and flowers and food; Patsy, who was to be a bridesmaid, wondered what she would wear. Tracy would have liked Allison to be a bridesmaid too, but it seemed this was not to be. Ryan was adamant that they get married before they set out to bring Allison and Derrick back.

Mrs Demant insisted that Tracy live at Sea View until the wedding, starting that very night. 'My future granddaughter will not sleep in that awful shack,' she said firmly.

'A strong-minded family I'm marrying into,' Tracy murmured, but with a smile. Already Mrs Demant and Patsy had found a firm place in her heart.

They talked a while longer, and then Ryan's grandmother, with a meaningful look at Patsy, said it was getting late.

'Time to retire, leaving you two love-birds to yourselves,' said Ryan's irrepressible sister. ' 'Night, brother dear. 'Night, Tracy, I'm going to enjoy having you as a sister.'

'I like them,' Tracy said when the door had closed behind them. 'I really like them.'

'I'd say the feeling was mutual.' Ryan came across to her, took her hands and drew her from the chair. 'How about a walk before I go back to Umhlowi?'

The night was hot, and sweet-smelling with the scent of jasmine and gardenias. Sea View had a huge garden, lushly and beautifully cultivated, and Tracy knew she would enjoy exploring it in the daytime. It was closer to the sea than Umhlowi, and the sound of the waves was a ceaseless roar.

They walked slowly, Ryan's arm around Tracy's shoulder, her own arm going around his waist. This was how they would walk together through the years she thought on a wave of happiness. Wrapped in a special togetherness. Talking, sharing the joys and problems of the day. Making love.

'Looking forward to Saturday?' Ryan asked.

'Oh yes. Are you?'

'You know the answer to that.' He stopped, and turned her into the circle of his arms. He held her loosely, but here and there their bodies touched, and Tracy felt a tingling that was becoming rapidly familiar. Ryan's arms began to tauten. Was this how it would always be between them? The awareness, the excitement, the desire to make love? Without having slept with Ryan, Tracy knew already that he would be a wonderful lover, passionate, possessive, considerate enough never to hurt her. And she would always want him, she could not imagine a time when she would not want him.

She pushed herself a little away from him so that she could look at his face. 'We know so little about each other.'

'Having second thoughts?'

The sight of his face, so rakishly handsome in the moonlight, caused her heart to do a little somersault. Somehow she resisted the urge to move back towards him again, to rest her cheek against his chest. 'You know nothing about me.'

'Wrong.' His warm breath fanned down towards her. 'I know that you're a whiz at painting trees. I know that you are able to sleep on dreadful mattresses, and that you never think of checking rain-water tanks before taking a shower.'

She laughed, the sound joyous on the hot air. 'Be serious!'

'Do you know what you're expecting of a man? Asking him to be serious when all he wants is to make passionate love to you?'

'Ryan . . .' she began, a little unsteadily.

'What do you want me to say, Tracy? I know that

you're lovely and desirable, that I want you in my bed at night. Every night. That you'll be an adorable wife, a wonderful mother for our children.'

Not a word about loving her. Four simple words—I love you, Tracy. Would he ever say them?

'There *are* things I should know. Ryan—your parents?'

'Killed in a motor accident.'

'Oh, darling, I'm sorry.'

'It was many years ago. Grandma moved in, brought us up. Patsy was a baby.'

'Your grandmother is quite a lady.'

'That she is. And she's taken a shine to you. You've never mentioned your father, Tracy.'

'He died quite a few years ago, too. Things haven't been easy for Mom.'

'She'll visit us often.'

'Yes.' She shifted restlessly in his arms. There was a question she had to ask, unwise though it might be. 'Who is Freda?'

'A neighbour. A close friend of the family.'

'A close friend of yours, Ryan?'

'At one time.' His arms dropped.

'Is there a Mr Antonis?'

'Freda is divorced.' His voice was harsher now. Part of Tracy was sorry she had brought up the subject, another part understood that there were things she had to know.

'I'm thirty-four,' Ryan went on. 'I told you I hadn't lived the life of a monk. There have been women.'

'I know that.'

'It's *you* I want now. Don't you understand that? Haven't I shown you?'

Relief was a lightening of the burden that had oppressed her since Freda's provocative embrace. 'You could show me again,' Tracy teased.

Ryan grinned down at her, the harshness gone. He was once more the handsome man she loved so much. 'I never resist an invitation from a gorgeous woman,' he growled, and then he was pulling her against him.

'It's you I want,' he repeated in a whisper as his hands went beneath the heavy hair to cup her head. 'Don't think of those others, Tracy.'

Their kisses were timeless, drugging, stopping all thought, stirring the senses. Tracy felt a strong heart beating in unison with her own, and as she was consumed by a sheer agony of wanting she wound her arms up around his neck and pressed herself against him. The shudder that ran through the strong male body told her just how much she inflamed him.

He lifted his head. 'Careful.' His breathing was ragged. 'You'll push me beyond control.'

'Perhaps it's what I want.'

'Abandoned girl.' He gave an unsteady laugh. 'Tracy, honey, we're being married in a few days. We'll wait 'till then. Go to bed now, my dearest, you may as well get some sleep because I might not let you sleep at all after Saturday.'

Next day Tracy went shopping. A wedding-dress, a veil, shoes. Could she find them so quickly? Yes, of course she could. She'd have been content with a pastel-coloured dress in a soft fabric, but Marie Demant's heart was set on a traditional wedding, and there was a part of Tracy that was glad. A traditional wedding, however simple, would be something to remember.

She would do the ground-work today, the trying-on, the looking around. But she would wait until her mother arrived to make the final purchases. They would go shopping together. Tracy, her mother and Mrs Demant. Anything else would be hurtful and disappointing.

It was going to be a busy day. Besides the wedding apparel, there were so many other things to buy. The clothes Tracy had brought with her constituted a survival wardrobe, a few basics that had been intended to see her through two or three days at the most. She had asked her mother to bring some of her clothes with her when she came to Sea View. But already she knew that as Ryan's wife she would need more.

Ryan had given her one of his cars, with directions about how to get to Margate, the nearest big town. 'You'll need money,' he said, putting his hand in his pocket.

'I have a cheque-book.'

'You're going to use your legacy?'

'Of course.'

'Tracy, you're going to be my wife, I want to buy you things.'

'And so you will. Be careful, Ryan, I might just spend everything you have.' She had laughed up at him, happy and secure in the fact that they could laugh together. 'These are my last few days as a single girl. Until we're actually married I'm going to use my own money.'

'Independent female,' he had growled, but good-naturedly. 'Don't go emptying the shops then. Leave me something to pay for.'

Her spirits were high as she took the coastal road to Margate. The sky was blue and cloudless and there was just enough of a breeze to take the edge off the heat and the clamminess from the air. There was little traffic, so that she could enjoy the scenery, the sparkling sea, the lagoons, the wild palms that grew everywhere.

She was smiling as she reached the city and began to look for a parking space. It was going to be a good day.

She spent some time looking at wedding-dresses, and discovered that if the selection was not as large as it would be in Durban, finding something pretty was not going to be difficult.

One dress was particularly lovely. Made of a heavy, creamy satin, it fitted snugly over high breasts, then flared gently away from the waist, gathering width and soft folds in its flow to the ground. The sleeves and a yoke that went up to the throat were made of a delicate lace, and the whole effect of the dress was romantically ethereal.

Tracy was tempted to take it, but she explained her situation to a willing sales-lady who was happy to put the dress aside a few days.

Leaving the bridal shop, Tracy began to look for other clothes. Tall and slender, she had a figure that was easy to fit, and her happy mood was a help. In no time at all she had found things she liked. Two elegant silk dresses, just right for the evening. Some casual clothes—three pairs of sleek designer-made trousers, a few lovely blouses, and a flared skirt in various shades of blue and green which reminded her of the ocean.

Until how she had always, of necessity, been careful how she used her money, but her uncle's inheritance had been an unexpected and rather wonderful windfall, opening up horizons previously beyond her orbit. Suddenly she had been able to entertain hopes of furthering her career, had dreamed of travel. But still she had been careful, had budgeted her every penny.

Today's spending-spree was something new. It was fun. The fact that she could spend what she wanted without remorse made her feel a little light-headed.

She was coming out of a shop when a husky voice said, 'Hello, Tracy,' and she turned to see Freda Antonis.

'Hello, Mrs Antonis.'

'Why so formal?' Freda was smiling. She looked so incredibly elegant that Tracy felt suddenly gawky.

'Freda,' she amended awkwardly.

The woman's eyes had gone to the parcels she carried. 'Shopping?'

'Yes. The wedding is just a few days away . . .'

The smile widened, showing perfect teeth without extending to the beautifully made-up eyes. 'Is Ryan with you?'

'He's at Umhlowi. I took his car.'

With no chance of meeting Ryan, Freda would lose all interest in her and be on her way, Tracy surmised. So she was surprised when Freda said instead, 'Why don't you join me for coffee?'

Coffee was the very last thing Tracy felt like having. She was searching for a polite way to say so when she was forestalled.

'All those parcels, you must be exhausted. I would think a coffee-break is just what you need.' Another smile. 'Besides, it will give us a chance to get to know each other.'

It was hard to refuse such a gracious invitation. 'A break would be nice,' Tracy acknowledged with a smile.

'Wonderful. There's a nice restaurant on the next corner.'

The restaurant was small and chic, and rather empty. They ordered coffee and a toasted cheese sandwich each, and made conversation. Freda did most of the talking. Small-talk, light and amusing. If Freda was good at it, Tracy was not. In the company of the sophisticated woman she felt like a schoolgirl, colourless and a little foolish. A little of the joy seemed to have gone out of the day.

Relax, she told herself. Try and relax. All right, so she's beautiful and you're no competition for her, and she was one of Ryan's women—but it's over. He chose you to be his wife. Hold on to the thought.

'Looking forward to the wedding?' Freda asked.

'Very much.'

'How old are you, Tracy?'

'Twenty-two.'

'The age I was when I married.' Bright eyes studied her, made her uncomfortable. Tracy took a sip of coffee, and shifted on her chair.

'Been shopping for wedding clothes?'

'I looked at some wedding-dresses. But I thought I'd wait and make the final choice when my mother gets here. I've a feeling she and Mrs Demant would like to see the dress before I take it.'

'Wise girl.' Was that malice in the bright eyes? 'Marie Demant will love that. And you.'

She's telling me something, Tracy thought, and she doesn't know that she's lost me.

'But you do have a lot of parcels. I gather you've been buying other clothes too?'

'Quite a few actually.' Tracy lifted her chin, wondering why she felt the need to be defiant. 'Dresses. Some rather nice trousers.'

'Marvellous,' Freda said with the smile that Tracy was beginning to dread. 'Of course, there's no sense in buying too much. I mean you can always get more afterwards.'

'Afterwards?'

'When you have your figure back.' A tinkling laugh this time. '*After* the baby is born.'

Tracy stared at her. 'There is no baby.'

'But there will be. Very soon.'

Anger stirred inside the girl. Instinct had told her there could be more to Freda's invitation than just friendliness. 'Is that what you think?' It was an effort to keep her voice low and controlled. 'That I'm pregnant?'

'Of course not.' The husky voice, calm and well-modulated, seemed to be mocking her. 'But you will be.'

'And if I do happen to become pregnant, is there anything wrong with that?'

'Not at all. It would be right in keeping with Ryan's plans. And his grandmother's.'

It was quite warm in the restaurant, but Tracy felt suddenly cold. 'I don't know what you're trying to tell me,' she said, 'but I don't think I want to hear any more.'

'Because you're frightened of hearing the truth?'

'I know the truth. Ryan and I want to be married. That's all there is at the moment.'

'I suppose you think he's in love with you?'

Of course. The words bubbled on Tracy's lips. Only to die there, unspoken. Ryan had never said he was in love with her. She looked at the other woman, feeling a little ill. 'I must go. I still have some things to do . . .'

'You *are* frightened.' A hand leaned over the table, detaining her. At the touch Tracy felt nauseated. Firmly she removed her own hand and put it in her lap.

'So he hasn't told you.' Malice mingled with concern in the sexy voice. 'Men can be so unfair, can't they?'

Hasn't told me what? Tracy's nerves felt raw. She wanted only to get out of this restaurant. But something kept her in her seat.

'Ryan wants a child.'

'That's not unusual. I want one too.'

'Marie Demant wants a great-grandchild. Ryan would do anything to please his grandmother.' Freda paused. 'You still don't understand, do you?'

Tracy wondered if she had ever disliked anyone quite so much. 'I do understand,' she said quietly. 'You're not happy about our marriage. You had a relationship with Ryan.'

'So you know about that.'

'It wasn't hard to guess after the way you behaved last night. Besides, Ryan told me about it.'

'He did?'

'He also told me that it was a thing of the past.'

Freda laughed, a low amused laugh that had Tracy sitting on the edge of her seat with discomfort. 'Oh, the things men say when they're after something. Are you a virgin?'

'That's none of your business.'

'You've just answered the question.' Freda's amusement deepened. 'Oh dear, why will men behave so stupidly, so unfairly? Ryan wants a child, Tracy. He wants it soon. That's why he's marrying you.'

Somehow Tracy found her voice. 'If all that you're implying is true. If you and Ryan . . . If he wanted . . . He could have married you.'

'He could not.'

'You're divorced.'

'You really have discussed me together. But Ryan just happened to leave out the important bits. You're quite right, Tracy, I'm divorced. My husband was a very wealthy man, I did very well out of him. But I lose it all if I remarry. It wouldn't be worth my while to marry Ryan. Now do you understand?'

'I must go . . .'

'You'll be doing well too, you know. Ryan is a rich man. You'll have every luxury you could want. Status too. And the affection of his all-important grand-mother, as long as you play the game right, which you seem to be doing. Waiting for her approval on your wedding-dress—Marie will adore that.'

'I don't want to hear any more.'

'It shouldn't matter too much that your husband will be enjoying himself with me on the side.'

Tracy sucked in her breath. 'He won't be.'

'You've just admitted you're a virgin. You've no experience.' Freda spread hands whose every nail was long and red and immaculately groomed. 'How on earth are you going to keep a man like Ryan interested?'

Tracy clenched her hands tightly beneath the table in an effort to maintain her composure. 'He's interested already. He's given every evidence of it.' She looked the other woman straight in the eye. 'You're jealous, Freda.'

'You're crazy.'

'No. Patsy said it last night, and she was right. Ryan said things were over between you, and I believe him. He'll be furious when I tell him the things you've been saying.'

'But you won't be telling him.' Freda gave her a look of disbelieving amusement. 'You're young, I know, but even so, you can't be quite so foolish.'

'You don't want me to tell him.'

'It's all the same to me. If you don't mind Ryan being defensive and aggressive, perhaps losing interest in you altogether, then go ahead and tell him.'

Tracy fumbled in her purse for some coins. 'Take this for the coffee. I have to go now.'

Head held high, she walked out of the restaurant. She knew that Freda's words had been lies. Just as she knew that Ryan wanted her for herself. True, he had never said that he loved her, but his taut body and his passion told of his desire every time that he touched her. She would not ask him about Freda again, he had already reassured her on the subject, and he did not have to defend himself twice. Besides, she believed him.

Nevertheless, the woman's spitefulness had had an effect on her. Instead of going on with her shopping, Tracy returned to the car, left Margate, and drove back to Sea View.

Lucille Galland arrived the next day. Ryan drove

Tracy to the station to meet her. Her mother was impressed with Ryan, Tracy saw right away. Also a little intimidated, though she had no reason to be, for Ryan was friendliness itself, showing none of the arrogance he had displayed towards Tracy at the start.

'So you're the man who swept my daughter off her feet,' Lucille said when Ryan was starting the car.

'Didn't Tracy tell you, Mrs Galland, that she was the one who did the sweeping?'

Lucille looked at him a little doubtfully, and then she saw his wicked grin, understood the joke for what it was, and a moment later they were laughing together.

Tracy felt her heart turn over with love for him. Since yesterday she had been imagining him with Freda, tormenting herself with images. Ryan and Freda in the pool, on the boat. Alone together. Ryan, superb in his brief swimming trunks, Freda, sultry and voluptuous, in the gold bikini. In every picture the bikini featured, for Tracy had no doubt now to whom the garment belonged.

'Right, Tracy?'

She blinked at Ryan, wondering at the question.

'It was you who did the sweeping off feet, wasn't it?'

His eyes were sparkling, and he looked so very handsome, and it was easy to return the smile. 'Rascal,' she teased back. 'You know which one of us is an expert with the broom.'

And then they were all three laughing, and Tracy knew it was time to banish Freda from her mind. Patsy had been right, the other woman was jealous. Maliciously jealous, so that she had been driven to hurt the girl who had succeeded in winning the prize she herself had been after. Ryan had said the relationship with Freda was a thing of the past, that was where it belonged, that was where Tracy would leave it.

Marie Demant was waiting for them at Sea View, as warmly welcoming as Ryan. 'I'm delighted to have Tracy as a granddaughter,' she told Lucille. 'And I'm so happy to meet you, Mrs Galland.'

Lucille was shown to her room, after which they all had brunch together, and then it was time to drive into Margate to see the wedding-dress. 'I feel we're rushing you, Lucille,' Mrs Demant apologised. 'You've only just arrived and you must be tired, but with the wedding so soon there's so much to be done.'

There was immediate agreement over the dress, as Tracy had thought there would be. Both Lucille and Marie were enchanted with it, and Tracy herself liked it even more than the first time she'd seen it. 'You'll be a beautiful bride,' Mrs Demant said, and Lucille dabbed at her eyes.

A veil was bought next, and then shoes. Flowers were chosen, sprays of orchids for Mrs Galland and Mrs Demant. Freesias for Patsy. An especially lovely bouquet for Tracy. The florist promised that the flowers would be delivered to Sea View early on Saturday morning. At last, it was time to leave Margate. There was more to do, but it had been a long day, and Ryan's grandmother was beginning to look tired.

It was only late that evening, when Ryan had driven back to Umhlowi, that Tracy was alone with her mother for the first time. Lucille, looking tired now too, had gone to bed, and Tracy came to her room with two cups of hot tea.

'Just what I needed,' Lucille said gratefully. 'I can't believe that it's not twenty-four hours since I left home, so much has happened.'

'It certainly has.' Tracy framed the question that had been on her lips all day. 'How do you like Ryan, Mom?'

'He's rather fantastic.' Her mother smiled at her.

'But I think you know that. You love him, don't you, darling?'

'So much.' It was not necessary for her mother to know that what Ryan felt for her was not love.

'I like them all. Mrs Demant. Patsy.' Lucille made a gesture. 'These people, Tracy, the way they live ... It's all so much more than I could have imagined. A little overwhelming.'

'But in a very nice way,' Tracy suggested.

Her mother nodded. 'Oh, yes.'

A mischievous smile touched Tracy's lips. 'Do you still think that Derrick was after Allison's inheritance?'

'No.' The smile vanished from Lucille's face. 'You still haven't spoken to Allison?'

'Ryan will take me to see her after the wedding.'

'I hope it's not too late.'

'It won't be. I've told you that.'

'I hope to God that you're right.'

A little curiously Tracy looked at her mother. 'I imagined today might have changed the way you felt about Allison and Derrick.'

'Not at all.'

'You've met the Demants. Aren't you happy for Allie?'

'I want you to get her back for me.'

The terminology struck Tracy as odd somehow. 'Mom—why?'

'We've been over all that. She's so young, Tracy. Only seventeen.'

'Almost eighteen,' Tracy said firmly. 'She will be eighteen by the time she and Derrick get married.'

'It's not right for her. Not yet.'

'Allie's young, Mom, I agree, but lots of girls marry at eighteen.'

Lucille moved restlessly beneath the sheets. 'I want you to bring her back to me, Tracy.'

To me. For me. Why did her mother use these words?

'Mom, why? If she loves Derrick . . .'

'She doesn't know what love is.' Lucille's voice was harsh. 'She thinks she's in love. She doesn't know what she's giving up.'

Tracy tensed. 'I don't know either.'

'A career! Her chance to be on the stage.'

At last Tracy understood. She wondered why it had taken her so long. 'Her dancing.'

'And her singing. All her life Allison's been working towards a stage career. How can she give it all up now, just to be married?'

'Perhaps it's what she wants.'

Lucille turned a distraught face. 'I've worked so hard so that Allie could have her lessons. She's good, Tracy, I know she is. And now, when success is within her reach—she could have a part in the musical, you know she could—she wants to throw it all up for a husband!'

'Perhaps it's what she wants,' Tracy said again.

'And I tell you she doesn't know what she wants.'

'Or perhaps,' Tracy said, and her voice was very gentle, 'it's just that *you* want it for her.'

There was a choked sound as Lucille covered her face with her hands. Tracy sat quietly, watching her mother, wishing she could alleviate her distress, knowing she couldn't.

In the last minutes things had become clear. Tracy had believed Allison's youth and her mother's distrust of Derrick Demant to be the only reasons she had been dispatched to bring her sister back. Now she knew better, and she was filled with an aching compassion for the young girl Lucille Galland had once been. A girl who had given up her own hopes for a stage career to be married. Given them up only temporarily as she had thought at the time. But fate had dealt her an unkind hand. Her husband had died young, leaving her with two small children to support.

It had been impossible for the young Lucille to return to the insecurity of stage work, to wait for weeks, maybe months, for a part to come her way. Had she found one, there would have been other problems, for there had been no extended family with whom to leave two little girls while she worked at night. And so Lucille had gone to work in a dress-shop, a job that was more mundane perhaps than the stage, yet infinitely more dependable.

Tracy had shown no signs of show-business ability, but Allison had begun to dance almost before she could walk. And her mother had encouraged her, had taught her all she knew, had spent more than she could afford on lessons. In her mind all the sacrifices had been worthwhile, for she had seen in Allison the star that she herself had never had a chance to be.

Would Allison have made it? True, there was a musical in which she had been offered a part. A small part, but small parts could lead to bigger ones, might allow an agent or a producer to discover her. Did her sister have that special quality that made a star? Tracy wondered now. Did she want to be one? Or was marriage to a man she loved more important to her?

None of these questions were ones she could have tossed about with her mother. At least not now. Lucille Galland could see only that a dream was being taken from her a second time, and she was desperately unhappy.

But the fact was that going after Allison had become for Tracy a different matter altogether. While her mother wept quietly into her hands, Tracy agonised over what to do. Did she have a right to interfere in her sister's life? No, said one part of her. Yes, said another.

For there was the matter of Derrick. Patsy had spoken of him as a lady's man, a Casanova who went from one girl to another, a weak person who was

seduced by every pretty face and lovely figure that
came his way. Ryan, though less eloquent, had spoken
about his brother in much the same way. If Derrick
was really a good-for-nothing, as Tracy suspected he
might be, then Allison could well be heading for
disaster. Tracy owed it to her sister to open her eyes
for her before she made a commitment from which
there was no retreat.

It did not matter that her reasons for wanting to
find Allison differed from her mother's. On Saturday
she and Ryan would be married. Then they would go
after her sister and Derrick.

CHAPTER EIGHT

FROM the moment Tracy flung open the curtains she
knew it was going to be a perfect day. The wedding
was to take place in the garden at Sea View, with
contingency arrangements in the spacious living-
rooms if there was rain. But the dawn sky, a misted
colour still, was cloudless.

Tracy thought Ryan might have liked to be wed at
Umhlowi, but Marie Demant insisted on Sea View,
and already Tracy knew that what was dear to his
grandmother's heart was important to Ryan.

The gardens had never looked lovelier. The roses
were in lush bloom. Magnolia and gardenia and a few
deep pink frangipani were an exotic backdrop for the
elegant clothes of the wedding-party. All this Tracy
took in, but only on the periphery of her vision. For as
she walked across the lawn, her long white dress
swishing the grass, the train held by Patsy, she saw
Ryan. And through the sudden wild joy in her heart
she saw nothing else.

He stood waiting for her, taller than any other man there, his face unexpectedly serious, a well-cut dark suit giving him a formal air that she had not seen before. Yet still the Ryan she knew and loved, a man of uncompromising strength and maleness, a man of power and authority together with a sexuality so potent that he set off crazy sensations in her every time she was near him.

As she walked across the lawn towards him, moving steadily towards the moment when their lives would be irrevocably joined, it seemed incredible that not quite two weeks earlier she had been unaware of his existence.

Slowly the gap between them narrowed. Behind her she heard Patsy's little gasp of excitement. All around her was the hush of the wedding guests. And in front of her was Ryan.

She came to him, and looked up, and met the warmth of promise in dark brown eyes. She did not know if he could see her own eyes through the veil that covered her face, but then he said very softly, 'Hello, darling,' and she knew that he did see them.

They turned their heads forward then, and the ceremony began. Minutes later they were husband and wife.

The next hour or two passed in a blur. Tracy was to remember only vaguely her mother's happy tears, her kiss and the whispered 'Be happy, sweetheart'; Marie Demant's warm hug accompanied by a similar command. The congratulations of the guests, most of whom she did not know. Patsy's excitement. The popping of champagne corks, and the platters of food. The talk and laughter that filled the air, a ceaseless hum that even drowned out the sound of the ocean.

One guest did stand out. Freda, magnificent in a silky sheath of bright red that seemed to be moulded to every curve of her body. Smile brilliant, she gave

Tracy a cool peck on one cheek, before asking, 'Mind if I kiss the groom?'

'Of course not,' Tracy said generously, too happy to dwell on the venom which had oozed from the other woman's lips the last time they had met.

Freda reached up to touch Ryan's lips with her own, the kiss she gave him very different from the one she had bestowed on his bride, but Tracy did not care.

'Congratulations, darling,' Freda said. 'May your marriage be fruitful—that is what you want, isn't it?'

Ryan looked down at her, his face impassive, the expression in his eyes difficult to read. 'It's what most bridegrooms want, I think.'

'But you want it especially. As does your grandmother.'

Ryan was silent. If the remark was meant to provoke him, he did not rise to the bait. He was not a man to be played with, the thought came to Tracy even through her happiness.

'I'm sure the lovely bride wants it too.' The smile that swept Tracy's face had not lost its brilliance, but the eyes were cold. 'Be seeing you, Ryan darling,' Freda said, and then she was gone, mingling easily with the other guests.

As Tracy watched her go she felt a sudden tremor of uneasiness. For just a moment the day lost some of its sparkle. Freda seemed to have a knack for making that happen.

Then an arm went around her waist, tightened, and Ryan said, 'Enjoy yourself, Tracy. This is *your* day.'

Ryan's way of letting her know that Freda was a nuisance, but that she was not to let the woman get under her skin. 'Our day,' Tracy said, looking up at him in sudden gratitude, and at the same moment the uneasiness vanished.

It was late afternoon when bride and groom quietly left the wedding party. They came to Umhlowi and

Ryan stopped the car on a rise where Tracy could see the house, and the orchards extending on all sides of it.

'My favourite time of the day,' he said softly. 'I wanted it to be the time of your home-coming.'

Tracy moved her eyes from the long white house, the roof golden now in the light of the setting sun, to the man at her side. Her husband.

I love you, she thought. I didn't know I could love anyone so much. Simply she said, 'I'm glad.'

As she moved towards him on the seat his arm went around her. He was bending to her at the same time as she reached for his kiss. A deep kiss, hungry, searching.

'I've been wanting this all day,' she said, when they drew apart for breath.

'Do you imagine I've been thinking of anything else?' His voice was ragged.

'Ryan . . .' She was lifting her mouth again, but the arm left her shoulder.

'Not now, my dearest. I want you too much to be able to stop. And I don't want to make love to you in the car, I want it to be in bed. Our bed.' He grinned down at her, his eyes wicked. 'I think I've earned that right at last.'

There was silence as they drove further. Tracy was still sitting close beside Ryan, their bodies touching from shoulder to thigh. She looked out of the window, but with little interest now. She was only aware of the longing that gnawed inside her, and her breathing was a little irregular. She did not look at Ryan, she did not have to; there was a tautness about him, and she knew why.

The house had a deserted air. Letitia, the housekeeper, was at Sea View where the wedding party was still in full swing. She had family near the village, and Ryan had given her the week-end off—for two days they would be quite alone.

'Just as we were at the start,' Tracy said, and Ryan grinned.

He did not park in the garage, but stopped at the front of the house instead. Then he got out, came around to Tracy's side, opened the door, and lifted her into his arms. He was kissing her as he carried her up the steps, a kiss that was unbroken as he pushed open the door with a shoulder, and carried her over the threshold.

'Remember when you carried me out of the pool,' Tracy said shakily, when he gave her a chance to speak.

'Do you think I could forget?'

'You were kissing me then too.'

'Till you pushed me away.' His arms tightened beneath her knees, and his breath was warm on her cheek. 'I'm not likely to forget that day, it was one of life's most frustrating.' His tongue touched a path around her lips, as feather-light as it was erotic. 'Unlike today, my dearest. Today is different.'

In the bedroom, just yards away from the shower where he had proposed to her, he put her down. His arms went around her, and for a long moment they held each other close. They did not kiss, did not speak, did not move. The only sound in the room was that of their breathing. And there was the beating of hearts that longed for the fulfilment each could give the other.

At last Ryan pushed his hand beneath the heavy fall of hair that hung loosely on Tracy's shoulders. 'I want you,' he said.

'You have me.'

'I want you in bed, with no clothes between us.'

It was what she wanted too. So much.

'Let's get undressed then,' she said, and put her fingers on the buttons of her dress.

'Not like that.' His voice was soft. 'I'm going to

undress you, my dearest. And I want you to undress me.'

Ryan was an expert, she realised, as he began to take the clothes from her body. He knew how to increase the suspense, how to extract the maximum enjoyment from each movement, each second. He did not seem to mind her innocence, appeared content that she followed where he led. And she learned quickly, partly guided by Ryan, partly by sheer female instinct.

When all their clothes were off he held her against him for a few seconds. She could feel his body taut against her, sensed the passion strictly controlled and yet aching to give way. And then he carried her to the bed and laid her on it.

For a long moment they looked at each other. She stared up at him, and she was not nervous. She could only think how much she loved him, how beautiful he was. As for Ryan, there was an expression in his eyes which she had never seen, something almost akin to worship. 'You're so lovely,' he groaned suddenly, and then he lay down beside her.

He covered her body with kisses. And Tracy, losing any inhibitions she still had, kissed him too, moving her body against his without restraint, letting her lips and hands go whenever they wished, revelling in the knowledge that this was just the beginning. Years of lovemaking lay ahead of them.

The longing that had welled in her in the car was like an ache now. She had never known loving could be like this. And then, when she thought she could bear the hunger no longer, he took her, gently, barely hurting her, so that she knew just how considerate he had been.

'You'll enjoy it more next time,' he said.

'It was wonderful just as it was,' she told him, letting him cradle her to him.

They made love once more, and this time Ryan was

not as gentle. As he took her to new heights Tracy felt
an absolute explosion of elation. Afterwards they lay
quietly together, limbs intertwined.

'Happy?' Ryan asked.

'So happy that if I were to die today I'd have no
regrets.'

His arms tightened around her. 'May you always
feel that way,' he said.

The next two days were spent at Umhlowi. Wonderful
days. Ryan did not work. Instead they swam in the
pool and luxuriated in the sun and ate the meals that
Letitia had left in the freezer for them. Above all they
made love, and each time was more fulfilling, more
exciting than the one before.

They saw nobody. Had Lucille Galland been able
to, she would have stayed longer at Sea View, but the
wedding had come at a time when the boutique was at
its busiest, and so, reluctantly, she had departed for
home early the next morning, promising to return for
a longer visit as soon as she could manage to arrange
some leave.

Marie Demant and Patsy stayed away from
Umhlowi. They knew that Tracy and Ryan would
want to be alone. Knew too that there was no rush.
There was so much time for the family to be
together.

Two days after the wedding Ryan and Tracy set off
in search of the runaways. The road they took was one
that was unfamiliar to Tracy. A road that was wild and
beautiful. Sometimes it ran beside the sea, affording
glimpses of golden beaches, lonely and with a look of
being unmarked by man; of stone bridges and sleepy
lagoons; of a succulent underbrush so thick that it
would be a hardy person—or a foolhardy one—who
would walk through it bare-legged. And then the road
would snake inland, and beyond the palms that

crowded each other near the tar Tracy would see orchards, and occasionally some sugar-cane, though as Ryan explained to her, the sugar-cane belt was really further north.

She sat close to Ryan—even after two days of being continually in his company she wanted to be near him—and she wound down the window and drank in the loveliness all around her.

'You're smiling,' she heard Ryan say.

'Am I?' Her voice was languid, she knew she was smiling.

'You've been smiling for miles.'

She turned to look at him. 'Married life must be agreeing with me.'

'Making love by a moonlit pool. What would your mother say if she knew?'

Tracy laughed, warming at the memory of the previous night. 'Are you going to tell her?'

For answer he took one of her hands, and dropped a kiss in its palm. 'You're an abandoned girl.'

'I have quite a teacher.'

He looked at her, and the expression in his eyes sent the blood racing through her veins. 'There is so much I want to teach you,' he said.

'You have a willing student,' she told him, mock-demurely.

She heard his hiss of breath. 'Two days isn't enough for a honeymoon. Why don't we leave Allison and Derrick to their own devices and go off somewhere on our own?'

Tracy's eyes clouded. 'I wish it was possible.'

'They'd be quite happy, you know. If your sister is anything like you, she's probably having a wonderful time with Derrick.'

'That's what I'm scared of.'

After a moment Ryan said, 'Allison is as good as eighteen. Why not let them be, Tracy?'

'I can't.'

'Wasn't your mother reassured once she'd met the family?'

'She liked you all so much. But Mom has her reasons . . .' Tracy looked out of the window. 'Ryan, tell me about Derrick. Is it true that he falls for every girl he meets?'

'Only the pretty ones.'

'Perfect faces and perfect figures, Patsy said.'

'That's been his story until now.'

'And he's never been really serious about any one of them?'

'He's never had time to be. Before he could feel serious about one girl the next one was on the scene.'

'Which is why you're so convinced that Allison must have resorted to trickery and corruption.'

Ryan waited a moment before answering. 'That is what I thought,' he admitted.

'Is that hesitation I detect in your voice?'

Her husband turned to her, and there was a smile in his eyes. 'Women are not the only ones who can change their minds, my dearest. I've begun to wonder if Allison is like you—because if she is it could account for the fact that my brother has behaved totally out of character.'

Tracy held her breath. Two days of marriage. Two perfect days of loving and laughing and sharing and talking. And still Ryan had never said that he loved her. Was he going to say so now?

But he had fallen silent. At last Tracy said, 'Derrick really is a Casanova then?'

Ryan laughed. 'But not a bad fellow for all that. Actually I'm very fond of my young brother.'

And why not? Derrick, it seemed, had charisma to spare. But more and more it sounded as if he was not the right man for Allison. Their marriage would never last. Just as well she was going after her sister, even though her reasons for doing so were different from her mother's.

'Tracy!' Allison's face was a picture of amazement as the car drew up at the beach cottage and she saw her sister get out of it. 'How on earth did you find me? Have you been to Umhlowi? I didn't know you'd met Ryan.' The words tumbled from her lips.

Tracy hugged her. 'There are lots of things you don't know. Ryan and I are married.'

'Married!' Allison cried. 'When?'

'Two days ago.'

'I don't believe it! That's just incredible! I mean, I had no idea that you two even knew each other.' Allison looked up at Ryan. 'When Derrick and I are married you'll be my brother in more ways than one.'

Tracy and Ryan exchanged wry glances, which were lost on Allison as she went on, 'I must call Derrick, he'll be as thrilled as I am.'

Tracy put out a detaining hand. 'Allie, wait . . .'

But Allison was already gone. A slender figure, pretty and tanned a deep brown after days in the sun. Tracy stared after her unhappily.

She turned to Ryan. 'Did you see her eyes?'

'As green as yours.'

'She's radiant,' Tracy said in a low voice. 'I've never seen her quite like this before. She's in love with Derrick.'

'Perhaps,' Ryan said slowly, 'you really should just let them be.'

She stared at him. 'You said the same thing in the car. Yet just a while ago your attitude was so different.'

'I told you I'd changed my mind. I think I like your kid sister.'

Obviously he didn't understand that it was not Allison but Derrick who gave Tracy cause for concern. She was searching for a tactful way of putting the thought into words when Allison and a young man emerged hand in hand from the cottage.

'Ryan!' Derrick clapped a delighted hand to his brother's shoulder. 'Allie says you're married. Is she joking?'

'She is not.' Ryan grinned. 'Let me introduce you to my bride.'

In some ways, Tracy saw at once, Derrick was a younger version of his brother. Much younger, for if Ryan was in his early thirties Derrick could not be more than twenty-three. The same dark eyes and hair, the same tall lithe figure, the winging eyebrows. The same potent sexuality. But there the similarity ended. At first glance Derrick seemed to lack the strength and the authority and the power that his brother possessed in such abundance. Perhaps she was judging him un-fairly, Tracy reproached herself, perhaps it was just his youth that put him at a disadvantage. And yet she had the feeling that even ten years earlier Ryan would have been something of the awesome person he was today.

Derrick's eyes sparkled as they skimmed Tracy from head to foot in a study that was thoroughly male and assessing. He was making no attempt to hide either his interest or his admiration.

'Very nice,' he said, as his gaze lifted once more to Tracy's face. 'Very nice indeed. My brother has spent all his life evading marriage, I can see how you would have made him think differently.'

Tracy couldn't resist a laugh. 'You and your brother have things in common then. Ryan also sees the female in the role of the seductress.'

'Does he now?' There was a gleam in Derrick's eyes as he turned to Ryan. 'Did Freda come to the wedding?'

'There were many guests at the wedding,' came the abrupt reply.

'Grandma must have enjoyed herself. And she'll

have another wedding to look forward to very soon. Which reminds me.' Derrick turned back to Tracy. 'I haven't even welcomed my new sister into the family.'

So saying he took her hand in his and bent forward to kiss her full on the lips. The kiss lasted only a second, but the hand held hers longer. It was Tracy who pulled away first.

'You must be thirsty,' Derrick said. 'Come into the cottage. I've laid in a stock of beer and lemonade.' He put an arm around Allison's shoulders. 'Do we have any cake left, pet?'

'If you haven't eaten it all by now.' Allison's merry laugh was a happy sound on the still air. 'This man of mine is an absolute glutton.'

It was mid-day. Too hot for the beach, so they made themselves comfortable on the cottage verandah instead. The sisters drank iced lemonade while the brothers sipped beer, and there was just enough cake left for four people.

The cottage was built into the cliff. The verandah was built at a height, giving it a spectacular view over the ocean. It was a lovely stone-floored area, with white cane chairs and rush mats and some rather lovely flowered ceramic tiles on one wall. But Tracy was in no mood to take it all in. For the present her mind was only on her sister.

Allison was definitely a girl in love. It was a love that showed not only in the radiant eyes which Tracy had noticed already. It was a love that she seemed to wear like a flag for all to see. It was there in the extra sweetness of her smile, in the lilt of her voice, most of all in the adoring glances she threw Derrick's way.

It was not hard to understand why Allison had fallen for him. The warm smile, the low teasing voice, the aura of male sexuality so like his brother's, all these made him intensely appealing. But Derrick was a flirt. Patsy had said so, Ryan had confirmed it. Now

Tracy had discovered the fact for herself. She had not imagined the unashamed scrutiny, nor the length of time he'd held her hand. Derrick, she thought, would always be a ladies' man, and the fact worried her intensely.

He was, as she'd suspected all along, a Casanova. He liked women, he liked to look at them, he liked to touch them. For the moment perhaps he imagined himself in love with Allison, so much so that he had decided to marry her. But even if Allison was the girl he loved now—infatuation was surely a better word for the emotion—how long could it last? Tanned and excited and radiant with love, Allison was more enchanting than ever. But the time would come when Derrick would grow accustomed to her prettiness; then when the next pretty girl came his way his attention would wander.

She was the right one to be condemning a man for his lack of love, Tracy thought wryly. Ryan did not love her either, anything he felt for her was purely physical. But she was older than Allison, old enough to have known what she was getting into when she married Ryan. Her eyes had been open, she had known that if she was settling for second best—for it would only be that while Ryan did not love her—she was prepared to accept it. But Allison would be going into marriage blind, and she would be destroyed.

'What brings you to the cottage?' Derrick asked at length. Tracy had been wondering when the question would come up. 'Surely not your honeymoon?'

'With you two to keep us company?' Ryan teased as he flicked a lazy glance at Tracy. Evidently he was leaving the answer to her.

'We came looking for you,' she said pleasantly.

'To get us to leave here?' Derrick did not sound surprised.

'Something like that.'

Allison sat up straight in her chair. 'We're not going.'

'Allie . . .'

The sweet face was set in stubborn lines which her sister recognised. 'We're staying here, Tracy.'

'Mom is worried about you.'

'So she sent you after me.'

Tracy hesitated. Then she said, 'I think it's best you come home.'

'Derrick and I are going to be married.'

'Without Mom? Without Derrick's family? Running off like this isn't the way to do things.'

'Would your mother have given us her permission and her blessing?' Derrick asked.

'Perhaps not her blessing. But once Allison's eighteen she couldn't have withheld her permission, you know that.'

'She would have made it difficult. It's better this way,' Allison said.

Tracy looked at her sister a long moment. She saw the defiant tilt of her head, the challenge in the lovely green eyes. Better to drop the conversation for now, she decided. Nothing would be achieved by continuing it.

Ryan must have been of similar mind, for he changed the subject, telling Derrick news of the farm, of the trees that Tracy had painted in his absence. In no time he had them all laughing.

'You're driving back today?' Derrick asked after a while.

'No, I think we'll stay a day or two. I keep forgetting how pleasant it is out here.' Ryan met his brother's sceptical gaze. 'It's a good chance for me to drive out to Jannie Landsman's farm. There's something I need to discuss with him.'

Perhaps it was true and perhaps it wasn't, but Tracy had the feeling that Ryan's basic reason for staying longer at the cottage was to give her a chance to talk again with Allison, and she was grateful to him.

In the late afternoon Tracy and Ryan took the path
to the beach. As they came on to the sand they kicked
off their shoes, slung them over their shoulders, and
began to walk hand in hand. The sun was setting and
over the sea the sky was spectacular, a brilliant palette
of gold and scarlet and vermilion. The tide was
coming in, the waves huge and a little fearsome in the
moment before they hurtled downwards in a wild
explosion of foam. Everywhere there were shells left
by previous tides, and never gathered because the
beach was so lonely that it could well have been
private, existing only for the enjoyment of the
Demants. The feeling of privacy was enhanced by
high dunes, and behind them the succulent underbrush
and the palms that seemed to grow everywhere on this
tropical stretch of the coast.

Normally Tracy would have enjoyed every minute
of the walk. The photographer in her would have
gloried in the shadings made by the dying sun; the
bride in her would have revelled in the intimacy with
her new husband, the happiness of seeing the foam
curl around their bare ankles, of knowing that
afternoon would blend into night which would bring
with it a very special intimacy of its own. But her
mind was not on the beauty all around her. It was on
Allison, on the potential mess that her sister was
getting herself into.

The hand that held hers gave it a squeeze. 'You're
very tense, darling. Can't you try and relax?'

Warming to the endearment, she looked up, and
thought how handsome he was. How could she help
loving him?

'I'll try,' she promised.

'Worried about Allison?'

'A bit.'

It was hard to put what she felt into words. Ryan's

loyalty would be with his brother. Until very recently his opinion of Allison had been low. True, it had changed, but she had no way of telling how much. So she had to keep her fears to herself.

'You don't want to see them married,' Ryan said.

'Not for a while at least.'

Ryan stopped walking, and Tracy stopped too. He turned her into the circle of his arms, and they stood close together for a moment. Then he took a step back and let a hand shape itself to the curve of a cheek. 'Playing God, Tracy?'

'I don't know . . .'

'It doesn't always work out for the best you know.'

'I have to try,' she said at last, in a low tone.

'I had my own reasons for distrusting Allison at the beginning. Care to tell me what you don't like about Derrick?'

If only she knew Ryan just a little better. She loved him, she loved him more than life itself, but as yet she didn't know him all that well. There were things that she could not say to him.

'I'm not sure,' she said slowly, 'if they're right for each other.'

'Perhaps you'll be more sure in a day or two. I meant what I said about staying a while longer.' He cupped her head with his hands and brought his lips down to hers. Fire stirred inside her, as it always did when he kissed her, and without thought she opened her mouth to him.

'Ah.' She felt rather than heard him laugh against her throat. 'That's better. Much better, my darling. Try concentrating on me and not on our stubborn siblings.'

She did just that. As they began to make love on the lonely beach all thoughts of Allison fled her mind. There was only Ryan and the wonder of the sensation that only he knew how to wake in her.

CHAPTER NINE

WITH the day so perfect, it was decided to have a braaivleis supper. While the men made a fire in the cottage garden, Tracy and Allison prepared a few things in the kitchen.

Tracy's limbs were still heavy with the lovely languor that had been with her since the lovemaking, but a part of her mind was starting to function once more. Though she and Ryan would be here a few days, her moments alone with Allison might well be fleeting. For a little while now she had her sister to herself.

'Have you given any thought to what I said earlier?' she began, as gently as she could.

Allison spun around, a wooden spoon flying out of her hand as she did so. 'About leaving here?'

'Yes.'

'Leaving Derrick?'

Tracy nodded.

'Forget it, Tracy! Just forget it! I love him, don't you understand?'

Oh yes, she understood. She knew what it was to be in love. To leave Ryan now would be to lose a part of herself.

'What have you got against him?' her sister demanded.

That he's a flirt and a perpetual playboy. That he'll squeeze every bit of love out of you that he can, and then tire of you and break your heart.

All of which Allison would deny. Already her eyes were sparkling with the light of battle.

'Derrick seems very nice,' Tracy said quietly. 'But Allie, you know why you ran off the way you did. You know why Mom's so set against the marriage.'

Allison pushed a hand through long glossy hair. 'She thinks I'm spoiling my chances of getting on the stage. Mom still thinks I'm going to be the star that she could never be.'

'Perhaps you could be.'

'We both know better than that. I dance and I sing but I don't have that special star quality.'

'You're losing a part in a play by being here with Derrick.'

'A part in a chorus.'

'Which could lead to bigger things.'

'And which probably would not.' Allison tossed the green salad so violently that Tracy marvelled that it did not land on the floor. 'Don't push me, Tracy. I know what Mom wants, what she's always wanted for me. It's true I was excited when I was offered the part, but then I fell in love and the play was no longer important.' She was silent a moment, then she said a little sadly, 'I know how much it means to Mom, but she has to accept that she doesn't have a second chance in me.'

Tracy was quiet. Every word that her sister had said was true. It was more or less the argument she herself had used with their mother.

Allison said fiercely, 'Derrick and I love each other. Nobody is going to stop us getting married.'

Which was one line of reasoning gone by the board. There was only one other, and that one had no chance of success. If Tracy so much as hinted at her suspicions of Derrick, Allison might never speak to her again, and she would marry him anyway.

Wisely she kept silent. The salads were ready and she put them on a tray and carried them outside.

It was a while since Tracy had partaken of a braaivleis in the moonlight. Ryan and Derrick were evidently experts at fire-making, for the flames had died low and the embers were grey, just right for braaing the meat. Steak with salads and hot buttered mielies made a delicious meal.

After the meal Ryan threw more wood on the fire and Derrick brought his guitar from the cottage. For a while he strummed softly, and then he began to sing, and after a bar or two Ryan sang with him, a song that had evidently been in the family a long time. Allison moved closer to Derrick and leaned her head against his shoulder, and Ryan's arm went around Tracy, holding her tight against the warmth of his body. And then Derrick played songs they all knew, and they all sang together.

The fire died once more and they did not revive it, but went into the cottage instead. Tracy was on her way to the room she was sharing with Ryan when Allison stopped her in the hallway, a challenge in her eyes. 'By the way, we don't sleep together yet.'

'I didn't ask,' Tracy said.

'But you wondered.'

Which was true. She had wondered just that.

Much later Tracy was still awake. Through the open window came the sound of the surf and the singing of the crickets. In the room there was the sound of slow steady breathing. After their time together on the beach Tracy had not thought Ryan would want to make love again, but he had done so very passionately and satisfyingly indeed.

Now he was sleeping. She lay on her side, feeling him all around her, for his body was shaped to fit with hers. An arm held her to him, the hand lightly cupping a breast. Tracy put a hand over his. They had been married three days. They should still be on their honeymoon, alone, with nothing to think about but themselves. It didn't seem fair that she should be burdened with a problem that appeared to have no solution.

It was no use appealing to Allison again. Her sister had made it clear that a stage career was of less importance to her than Derrick. She would not listen if Tracy said a word against him, that was clear too. There had to be another way.

It came to her so suddenly, that she sucked in her breath. Could she pull it off? Dare she?

For the next hour she thought about it, intrigued one moment, doubtful the next. In theory it *could* work. In practical terms it would be a matter of timing and opportunity.

Incredibly both timing and opportunity presented themselves the very next day.

They were sharing a lazy breakfast on the cottage verandah when it turned out that each person had different plans for the day.

'Doesn't that sea cry out to be fished in?' Derrick said.

Ryan grinned. 'Lazy sod. I thought I'd take that drive over to Jannie Landsman's.'

'Lazy indeed,' retorted his brother with mock indignation. 'You will eat your words tonight, together with a truly delicious fish.'

'We'll keep you to it, darling,' Allison laughed. 'I'm off to the dorpie to stock up on some groceries—I'll be sure to cross fish off my list.'

'Like to come along?' Simultaneously Ryan and Allison asked the same question of Tracy.

She hesitated only a moment. 'I don't think so.' She pretended to stifle a yawn. 'I feel a bit lazy myself this morning. Perhaps I'll go to the beach for a while.'

She watched Allison check her list, and asked, 'How long will you be away?'

'About an hour.' Her sister looked up at her. 'Sure you don't want to come?'

'Quite sure.' Guilty though she felt, she reminded herself that opportunity seldom knocks twice.

She watched them all go their separate ways. Derrick first, rod in hand, taking the path to the beach. Then Ryan driving off in his car, and a little later, Allison pedalling away on one of the cottage bicycles with a wire shopping-basket slung above the back wheel.

Tracy went back into the cottage. On her shopping-spree in Margate she had bought herself a bikini—not as sultry a garment as the one she'd worn on her first day at Umhlowi, but an outrageous piece of nonsense all the same. Something to wear when she was alone with Ryan.

She chose to wear it now.

Carefully she watched the time. An hour, Allison had said. Timing was all-important. Tracy must be neither too early nor too late.

Nervousness was making her jittery. All females were seductresses, thought the Demant men. It was a role Tracy had never played before, and she knew it would not come easily to her now.

At last it was time to go to the beach. Where the path gave way to the sand she stopped.

Derrick stood on an outcropping of rocks, rod in hand. She watched him a moment, then she kicked off her sandals, slipped off the shirt she'd put on over her bikini, and made her way nearer him.

'Derrick!' she called, when she realised that his concentration was on his rod and line, and that he had not seen her. 'Derrick!'

He turned, his face brightening when he saw her. 'Why, Tracy.'

She had adopted a model's pose, shoulders at a slight angle, one foot pointing outwards, the other just slightly behind it. The pose of a seductress? She did not know, and her mirror had not given her the answer.

Derrick was looking hard at her, and it seemed to her there was interest in his gaze.

She motioned to him. 'Come on down.'

After a moment he took a few steps towards her. 'Want something?'

'I'm going to sunbathe. It's lonely without Ryan and Allison. Why don't you join me?'

A glance that was totally male, half-arrogant, half-insolent, swept her from head to foot. Somehow she managed to keep her pose, and was glad that he was just a bit too far away to see the warmth in her cheeks.

'Why not?' was Derrick's casual response.

She did not wait while he reeled in his line and picked up his gear. She walked a little away from the rocks and spread her towel on the sand. As she arranged herself, elbows supporting her at the waist, one leg out-stretched, the other slightly bent, she noticed Derrick coming towards her.

It was working!

But what she felt was not triumph, it was sheer panic. This much she had rehearsed. From here on she would be ad-libbing her role. How far she would be called on to go she had no way of knowing. Thank God for the fact that Ryan was safely out of the way. She could only hope that her timing was right, and that Allison would appear before things had a chance to get too far out of hand.

As he squatted beside her she saw that the eyes that went over her almost bare figure held a gleam. 'So you felt like some company.'

She smiled at him from beneath her lashes. 'A girl doesn't like to be alone.'

'I'd have thought you'd have had very little time to be alone since you were married.'

His voice was polite enough, but there was something, the merest nuance, which she could not quite explain. She controlled the ripple of uneasiness.

'Very little time,' she acknowledged with another smile.

God help me, Allison, you may hate me for this, but I'm doing it for you.

'Why don't you tell me about yourself, Tracy?' he suggested after a moment.

Derrick wanted to *talk*? Somehow the scene was taking on a very different slant to the one she had visualised. What had she hoped for? Well, that she would be in his arms, and that Allison would appear in the crucial moment before she found herself having to surrender to his kisses. That kind of thing happened in movies, she acknowledged to herself now, but in real life, when you chose a scenario, sometimes you found yourself with more, or less, than you had bargained for.

She shrugged a bare shoulder. 'There's not much to tell.'

'I think there's quite a lot,' Derrick said softly.

Feeling even more uneasy than before, she said, 'If it's my life-story that you want, I'll be happy to tell it to you.' She darted him another smile. 'But I'm going to soak up some sun while I'm about it.'

So saying, she turned over on her stomach. A quick glance at her watch told her that Allison should have appeared by now.

'There's some sun-tan oil in my bag over there,' she said to Derrick. 'Be a pal, will you? Just undo the back of my bra and put some oil on my back.'

There was a moment of silence. She wished she could see Derrick's face.

'I really do want an even tan,' Tracy said, struggling to keep the uneasiness from her tone.

'As you like.' As Derrick unclasped the tie at her back, Tracy thought his fingers brushed purposely along her warm skin, and a feeling of revulsion shivered through her. Ryan should be doing this—only Ryan. But there was method to her behaviour. Some time in the future, when Allison had got over her hurt, she would be glad that she had found out in time that Derrick was nothing more than a philanderer.

'I can't reach my straps,' she murmured.

He drew them from her shoulders, and then he had picked up the bottle and was dropping oil on her back. A picture came into Tracy's mind, Ryan oiling her back on the deck of the yacht. And she was glad that he was not here to see her now.

Hurry Allison, please hurry. The fingers on her back were expertly sensuous, she was not the first girl Derrick had oiled, nor would she be the last. He was close to her, she could feel his thighs touching her bare skin, and he was making no effort to speak—somehow his silence was unnerving.

Panic welled inside her. She had started something with no clear idea of how it was going to finish, or where. All she could think of was her sister, wishing she would come soon. There was no need for Tracy to be wrapped in Derrick's passionate embrace. Allison could be fiery when provoked, the mere sight of her fiancé in this very intimate scene with her sister would be enough to bring out her feelings of anger. After that Tracy would be able to warn her about Derrick, and the chances were that she would be believed.

Long fingers began to rub oil into her shoulders. 'This is how you like it?' Derrick asked languidly.

'Uh-huh,' she murmured in a voice that was entirely foreign to her.

'Playing God, Tracy?' Ryan's words came back to her unbidden. She was beginning to feel more and more uncomfortable. Was wishing she had never started this. Part of her told her she was doing the right thing—Allison had to be rescued from a man who would bring her nothing but unhappiness. But there was a part of her that cautioned that she was getting mixed up in something that did not concern her.

'I suppose you want oil on the backs of your thighs too?'

'. . . Yes.'

This was awful! She hated the feel of Derrick's hands on her body. Hated what she was doing. Wished she knew where it would end. Wished she was the kind of person who could handle it.

Quite suddenly the hands on her thighs ceased moving. Seconds later a pair of legs were in Tracy's vision. Male legs, the calves taut and powerful. The breath stopped in Tracy's throat, and for a moment she felt so weak that she thought she might faint.

'Ryan!' She jerked upwards to a sitting position, remembering in the nick of time that her bra was open, clutching it protectively to her breasts. 'Ryan, what are you doing here? You said you'd be gone all morning . . . That you . . .' Her voice faltered and the words trailed away.

Ryan's face was an icy mask. Only his eyes seemed alive as they flicked her with contempt.

'You've been to Jannie and back?' Derrick asked disbelievingly as Tracy pulled her straps back over her shoulders, then reached behind her to fasten the clasp of her bikini—no easy feat with fingers that were suddenly as insubstantial as jelly.

'I didn't get to Jannie.' Ryan looked from Tracy to Derrick. 'I'm afraid there's been an accident.'

'An accident?' Tracy looked up at him, feeling a sudden shiver of fear.

Ryan's face was expressionless. 'Allison. She was knocked down by a car.'

Derrick swore hoarsely as he jumped to his feet and grabbed Ryan's arm. Tracy tried to stand, and found that her limbs refused to move. It was as if her brain had all at once lost its ability to send the necessary messages to her muscles. She could only look at her husband in horror. She opened her mouth to speak, and the words did not come.

Derrick spoke them for her, his face ashen beneath his tan. 'Where is she? Is she . . . is she dead?'

'She's alive.' Ryan put a hand on Derrick's arm. 'Unconscious but alive.'

Somehow Tracy found her voice. 'She'll be all right?'

'She *has* to be,' Derrick groaned out, without waiting for Ryan's answer.

'It's too early to tell. She was being taken to hospital when I left her. I came back to fetch you both.'

Derrick passed a dazed hand in front of his eyes, and Ryan put an arm around his shoulders. 'Steady, lad. I'll be with you.'

'Ryan . . .' Tracy looked up at her husband, her eyes anguished, pleading.

'Get dressed,' he commanded briefly. 'Then we'll go.'

He stretched out a hand to her, seeming to understand that she could not manage to lever herself from the ground alone. But the hand was cold, the hand of a stranger. And even through her despair Tracy realised that Ryan's compassion was only for his brother. After the scene he had interrupted, he had none left for her.

Back to the cottage they went, Derrick to change out of his wet fishing gear, Tracy out of her bikini. Neither of them took more than a few minutes to pull on some clothes. And then they were in Ryan's car, taking the road to the hospital.

Ryan talked as he drove, tersely, telling them what they had to know. He had been on his way to Jannie Landsman, had remembered a balance-sheet he'd left at the cottage, was driving back to fetch it when he'd come on the accident. It had happened by then. Allison was lying on the side of the road, where she'd been knocked off her bicycle by a car coming around a blind bend. The driver was with her, he had covered the unconscious girl with an old blanket he'd kept in the boot of his car. A passing fisherman had gone to phone for an ambulance. Ryan had waited for the ambulance, had seen the crew lift Allison on to a stretcher, had learned where they were taking her. Then he had returned to the cottage in search of Tracy and Derrick.

And a fine scene he had come upon. Tracy cast an unhappy glance at her husband. His hands held the wheel with unnecessary tightness. A tightness that extended to his corded throat. His profile was like stone. Clearly he had misunderstood the nature of the scene on the beach, and now was not the time to explain it to him.

Was it only yesterday that they had travelled this road from Umhlowi? She had been close beside him, his arm had been around her shoulders much of the time. Now she sat huddled against her door. The stretch of empty seat between them seemed almost ominously impersonal. It might have been a brick wall that had been erected to keep them apart. It should have been an easy thing for a wife of a few days to slide across that space, to lean against her husband and beg for his love and his sympathy and his understanding. But another glance at the forbidding profile told her that to cross the space would be as hazardous as crossing an uncharted mine-field.

Turning in her seat she looked at Derrick. His face was still very pale, and he looked tight and shaken. He would have been inhuman had Allison's accident not touched him, but to see him quite so distraught came as a revelation. Impulsively Tracy stretched over the seat and put out a hand to him. His eyes met hers for a moment, and then he moved his head quite deliberately and looked out of the window. After a moment she turned forward once more, and dropped the proffered hand into her lap.

They reached the hospital, and almost before the car had stopped Derrick had opened his door and was running up the steps. Tracy waited for Ryan. Inside her every nerve was quivering with tension. There was the terrible worry about Allison. And there was Ryan, as taut and granite-faced as he'd been on the beach.

'Ryan, about what you saw . . .' she began unhappily.

'Don't even try to explain,' he said, very pleasantly.

His tone chilled her. 'It wasn't what you might have thought.' She put an impulsive hand on his arm.

As if her touch offended him, he shrugged her hand away. 'Now really isn't the time to talk. Don't you want to find out about Allison?'

Said so coldly, so ominously. As if to imply that she did not care about her sister. Oh Ryan, it doesn't take very much to hurt your precious male pride, does it? Would it be any different if you loved me? Would your trust in me be such that you'd know there must be a reason for what you saw?

Allison was still in the operating theatre. Derrick was in the waiting-room, his eyes red-rimmed, his hair dishevelled from the many times he had pushed his hand through it. He was pacing up and down, his face distraught.

Tracy ran to him. 'Any news yet?'

'Nothing! Just a nurse who told me to sit down and be patient.' He made a savage gesture. 'Patient, my God! This is so frustrating!'

'I'll get us some coffee,' Ryan said.

Tracy sat down. She picked up a magazine, tried to leaf through it, only to put it down again. She could not read. She could think only of Allison. Allison laughing about the fish that she would strike off her shopping-list. Allison pedalling away on her bicycle, her fair hair blowing like a scarf behind her.

How long had her sister been in the operating

theatre? Time seemed to be measured by Derrick's pacing. Up the room and down again.

Her head jerked as a doctor came into the room. In an instant she was on her feet. 'Miss Galland's relatives?'

'Yes!' Tracy's throat was so tight that it hurt to speak. 'How is she?'

'You are her . . .?' The doctor looked at them inquiringly.

'Sister,' Tracy said.

'I'm her fiancé,' Derrick put in tersely. 'How *is* she, doctor?'

'The operation is over. She's in the recovery room. I think she will be all right.'

'Thank God!' Two simultaneous exclamations.

'She's had some painful injuries. A few cracked ribs. A broken leg.'

'They'll heal, won't they?' Tracy asked anxiously.

'They will. But the leg suffered a rather awkward break, I'm afraid.'

Tracy was caught by something in his tone. 'Are you saying she won't walk again?' Her voice was anguished.

'She will walk but it's too early to be definite about anything. There will be some permanent scarring. And she may walk with a limp.'

'When can we see her?' Derrick demanded.

'In a while. She's in the recovery room now. It will be a while before she's sufficiently over the anaesthetic to talk.'

'We'll wait,' Derrick muttered.

'There is one other thing.' The doctor hesitated, compassionate eyes going from Derrick to Tracy, then resting on Derrick again. 'There has been some internal injury. Nothing that will impair her life. But Miss Galland may be unable to have babies.' He hesitated again, and through her grief Tracy understood that this was not easy for him. 'I'm sorry to break all this to you, but sometimes it's better for people to know the facts.'

He left the room. Tracy looked helplessly at Derrick, then went back to her chair. She thought that Derrick would resume his angry pacing, but he slumped down beside her, and put his head in his hands.

Through her unhappiness her heart went out to him. He was taking the whole incident much more seriously than she would have given him credit for.

She put her hand on his arm, and unlike Ryan he did not push her away. 'Are you all right?'

'Yes. My God, Tracy, I should never have let her go.'

'Don't be silly.' She made an effort to speak firmly. 'It was an accident. You can't let yourself feel guilty.'

He looked up, his face haggard. 'You feel terrible too, don't you?'

Her voice caught. 'Yes.'

They were quiet a few moments. Tracy shifted restlessly in her chair. There was something she had to know. A cruel question perhaps, but, like the doctor, she understood there were things that had to be said.

In a low voice she asked, 'Will this make a difference?'

Lifting his head Derrick looked at her, dazed and without comprehension.

'Allison's injuries. I'm sorry, Derrick, but I have to know.'

'What are you talking about?'

This was harder than she had expected. Different too. 'You heard what the doctor said—will it make a difference?'

A strange expression came into his eyes. 'I think you're asking whether Allison's injuries will change the way I feel about her.' And when she did not answer. 'I love her. I love Allison. Dammit, Tracy, don't you understand?'

She stared at him numbly. Derrick the Casanova, the ladies' man, Derrick who was interested only in girls with perfect faces and perfect figures, was talking quite passionately about love. The one word that had never crossed his brother's lips.

'She may limp.'

'So what?'

'And she may never give you children.'

Something moved in Derrick's throat. 'What the hell are you trying to do, Tracy? Turn me against Allison? I love her! Sure I would have liked children. But what matters most is Allison. She's going to be my wife, and like it or not, you'd better understand it.'

Her eyes blurred with sudden tears. 'I do understand,' she whispered over the painful lump in her throat. 'And I'm glad. So very glad.'

There was something else she understood. She had acted rashly to save her sister from a marriage she had thought was doomed to disaster, when all the time it was not. Derrick and Allison loved each other. Though he would never know it, Derrick had just passed a test.

Tracy had put herself out on a limb to rescue Allison, when her sister had never needed rescuing. And the result could well be harm to her own marriage. A temporary harm, she tried to reassure herself, for she would explain to Ryan all that had happened, and he would understand. Of course he would understand.

The object of her thoughts walked into the waiting-room, styrofoam cups of coffee in his hands. She met his eyes as he gave her a cup, and saw that they were hard. Her anguished expression, the silent plea she sent him, produced no softening. And suddenly her confidence in her marriage was a fragile thing indeed.

She had known there would be a reckoning. It came later that night. Much later.

They had waited at the hospital until Allison had regained sufficient consciousness to recognise them and to say a few words. She had been able to tell them a little of what had happened. She had been pedalling in the middle of the quiet country road never expecting to meet a car. It had come upon her suddenly, and she had been knocked from her bicycle. There had been fault on both sides, Tracy knew. Ryan had told them the driver had been in a state of shock after the accident.

They did not talk long. Allison was beginning to feel pain, she was also very sleepy. Tracy left the room with Ryan. At the door she turned, and saw Derrick kissing her sister very tenderly on the lips.

They returned to the cottage to collect their belongings, and then had driven through the night back to Umhlowi, for the cottage was further from the hospital than the farm, and it did not have a telephone. Besides, whatever happiness there had been at the cottage was gone—there was no reason to stay there longer.

The first thing they did on their return to Umhlowi was to make phone-calls. One to Mrs Demant. The other to Lucille Galland. After the first moments of shock, Lucille said that upon Allison's discharge she must be brought back to Durban. It was a request which Tracy had anticipated, she had already discussed it with the Demant men, and she had her answer ready. As gently as she could, she explained to her mother that Allison would be best off at Umhlowi. With Lucille spending most of her day at work, a nurse would have to be hired to look after Allison. If she stayed at Umhlowi she would have Tracy's full-time attention. And besides, there was Derrick. It had taken an accident to bring home the fact that Allison and Derrick were right for each other, Tracy thought wryly, and the hand that held the phone to her ear shook.

Her mother gave in at length. Tracy promised to give her a daily report, and Lucille said that she would come to stay with them just as soon as she could arrange for somebody to fill in for her at the boutique.

Tracy's legs were weak as she made her way back to the living-room. Both men were there. Derrick staring moodily into a drink, and Ryan pouring one for himself. He asked Tracy what she would have, and she asked for a brandy. Ryan, who had never seen her drink, raised his eyebrows, but not a word passed his lips as he handed it to her.

Sitting down in a deep leather chair, Tracy closed her eyes and took a sip of the brandy. The alcohol was like fire in her throat, in a moment she felt the warmth of it burn her chest, her arms, her hands. She hated the taste, but she took another sip notwithstanding. She could not have said why she wanted it, except perhaps that she was so weary as to feel quite ill after one of the longest and hardest days she could remember.

And something told her—with a sureness that made the hairs on her neck stand on edge—that the day was not over.

She sensed rather than saw Ryan go to Derrick and talk with him quietly. Ryan's sympathy was all with his brother. It was true that Derrick had suffered a terrible shock. He loved Allison and he was deeply unhappy. But was there no compassion for Tracy? It was as if, since the moment when Ryan had come upon them on the beach, Tracy had ceased to exist for him. If he understood her despair there was nothing in his manner to show it.

At length Derrick lurched to his feet and said good night. Tracy glanced at her watch. It was nearly midnight. She looked at Ryan. 'Time for bed?'

The eyes that flicked her did not belong to a new and loving husband; they were those of a stranger.

CHAPTER TEN

TRYING to control a shudder Tracy put down her glass and walked without a word out of the living-room and into the bedroom. She was so tired that she had to push herself to brush her teeth and get undressed.

She came out of the bathroom to find Ryan in the bedroom. It was obvious that he had been waiting for her. The door was closed, and he was leaning lightly against it. Something in his eyes, in his bearing, made her think of a predator getting ready to close in on its prey. A pulse beat suddenly and hard at the side of her throat as she had a sensation of being trapped. She was being absurd, she told herself a moment later. Fanciful. She was in her own bedroom, with her husband who had every right to be here with her.

But he was not the husband she knew, she understood that too. There was a wildness in his face and in the eyes that ravaged her body. The look of power and strength that was with him always was enhanced, as was the air of sexuality. She had never seen him look quite so attractive. Or so dangerous.

Without thinking what she was doing she lifted her hands to shield breasts that were visible beneath the transparent shimmer of a silk nightgown.

As if the action triggered something inside him, his lips curved derisively and he took a step away from the door.

'Such modesty,' he mocked. 'I saw you in less this morning.'

Even at the start of their acquaintance, when he had treated her with scorn, there had not been quite this hardness in his voice, this note of utter dislike and contempt.

'You've seen me with nothing on,' she conceded steadily.

'So I have. The blushing bride. The innocent virgin. Passionate yet virtuous. So imbued with out-dated morals that she had to be married before she could surrender her precious virginity.'

'Stop this!'

'A virtuous slut. Mrs Ryan Demant, a virtuous slut. To think that I fell for it.'

'I don't want to hear any more.' She put her hands over her ears.

Only to have them torn roughly away.

'You'll hear what I have to say, my darling wife. You've set the terms all along, haven't you? That sweet innocence had me fooled, I admit it. I didn't know I was playing into your hands all the time.'

'Oh God, Ryan, stop it, please stop it.'

'What was it that attracted you to me? My money or my body?'

He was gripping her hands, holding them between their two bodies. He was so close to her that she could see the violence in his eyes, the tension in the skin that stretched over his cheekbones like a mask about to snap.

She was really frightened now, but she could not let him know it. 'You're drunk,' she snapped.

'And that offends you?' A jerk of his hands brought her even closer against him, so that she could feel the tautness of his body—a tautness that had nothing to do with love or passion.

'Yes.'

'Well, isn't that something. My innocent bride is offended by my drunkenness. You polished off your own brandy in quick time I noticed.'

'Only one,' she defended herself. 'Nothing wrong with that.'

'Except that you never showed that side of yourself until today either.'

'I don't drink, Ryan. I was upset about Allison.'

'Ah, Allison. I wondered when you were going to bring her into it. And Derrick. What will Allison say when she knows you can't wait to get the man she loves into bed?'

'That's not true!'

'So you deny that you were trying to seduce him this morning?'

'No. At least . . .' She looked at him helplessly. 'Ryan, I told you at the hospital that we had to talk.'

'You wanted to explain,' he said mockingly.

'Yes!'

'A waste of energy.' His tone was crisp. 'My eyes took in any explanation you might dredge up.'

'There was a reason for what I did,' she said despairingly.

'I've no doubt you've managed to think of one by now.'

'Ryan, please . . .'

He pushed her from him, so abruptly that she fell backwards against the bed. 'I don't want to hear it. Don't degrade us both further by trying to explain what happened, Tracy.'

She felt ill. 'Then where do we go from here?'

'Where do you think?'

'I suppose . . .' She stopped, wetting lips that were so dry that it was an effort to speak the words that would end everything she held dear. 'I suppose our marriage is over.'

Something moved in his jaw. 'I didn't say that.'

'You despise me. You don't trust me.'

He came to the bed and looked down at her, tall and lithe and aggressively male. 'No, I don't trust you.'

'Then I'll leave here. I'll go tomorrow.'

'You will not.'

She stared at him uncomprehendingly. 'It's the only way.'

'It's no way at all. For one thing, Allison will be back here soon. She'll need you to look after her.'

She had forgotten Allison. In the passion and unhappiness of the moment she had actually forgotten her sister. What's happening to me? she wondered despairingly.

'You're right. I'll stay till she's well.' She didn't know what made her add, 'You said "for one thing".'

Ryan did not answer. He just stood looking at her. She wanted to shield herself again, but pride came to her rescue. She would not grovel in front of him.

'For one thing?' she prompted him.

'It really doesn't matter,' he said softly. 'Just understand that there's no walking out. A few days ago you made some vows.'

'They don't apply any longer.'

'They apply. You're bound to me forever, Tracy.'

Why? Why? He hated her, he didn't trust her, yet he spoke of forever. The answer came to her suddenly.

'You're thinking of your grandmother.'

He did not answer. It didn't matter. She had her answer. If Ryan did not love Tracy, he did have very strong feelings of loyalty for his grandmother. Freda Antonis had explained that.

'I'll stay,' she said tiredly. 'But we'll be married in name only. It's what we both want. Leave me now, Ryan.'

'This is where I sleep.'

Slowly, deliberately, he unbuckled his belt.

'Then *I'll* go,' Tracy said, averting her eyes. 'There

must be a bed that's made up in one of the guest rooms.'

'You'll stay right here. In this bed.'

'No!' She shrank from him as he came towards her. 'Keep away from me.'

'Why? You tried to seduce Derrick this morning, and you didn't get what you wanted. You must be feeling awfully frustrated.'

'Don't touch me!' she hissed as he lowered himself on to the bed.

'I'll touch you whenever I like.' In a quick movement he pinned her down and rolled on top of her.

The minutes that followed were an agony, for there was no love in the act. Tracy was roused, stirred. Even in her state of fatigue it seemed that she was incapable of not wanting Ryan, of responding to his touch. But throughout she was aware that he was using her. That his only sensation was lust.

He rolled away from her at length, and soon the sound of his breathing filled the room. Tracy, so tired that every limb was aching, did not sleep. She lay as far from Ryan as she could, her eyes fixed on the open window. She felt numb and drained. Empty.

And she knew that in the months ahead—she could not allow herself to think in terms of years or she would go mad—there would be emptiness in abundance.

In the next weeks Tracy drove often to the hospital, usually at times when she knew that Derrick would not be there. She still felt awkward in his company, uncertain how to face him, what to say to him. The morning on the beach was still too vivid in both their minds, and she knew now that she could not explain to her brother-in-law why she had acted so wantonly. He would be very hurt, and she did not want to hurt him.

That he loved Allison became clearer all the time.
More so when they brought her sister home at last,
and Tracy was able to observe them together. The
love that flowed between them was something so
special that there were times when she found herself
actually envying her sister. Allison's injuries were
mending. There was no doubt that she would be able
to walk, it was only a matter of time. As for the fact
that she might not be able to have babies, that was
something she would have to learn to cope with. It
would not be easy, but she would accept it because
Derrick's love seemed to give her an emotional
strength at which Tracy could only marvel.

That Derrick was the right man for her sister she no
longer doubted. Even his reputation for being a
Casanova began to resolve itself in her mind. It was true
that Derrick enjoyed women. That he had been enjoyed
in return. There was something intensely charismatic
about him. How to explain the hand that had held hers
too long, the eyes that had assessed her with such
interest? Habit, most likely, Tracy decided. Derrick was
one of those young men who sowed their oats very
thoroughly when they were young. It did not mean that
he would continue to sow them as he grew older; nor did
it mean that he could not remain in love with just one
woman. Indeed, in contrast to his older brother, Derrick
was showing in every way possible just how much love
he had in him to give. Tracy took on the duties that
caring for her sister entailed willingly. It was so good to
see Allison looking better. It was also good to have her
living in the same house, for she knew that without her
sister she would be very lonely.

Things had not improved between Ryan and
herself. They ate their meals together, they slept in the
same room, and when Ryan was in the mood they
made love. Love? It had never been love, at least not
for Ryan. It had always been something physical. But

there had been a time, all too short a time, when what there was had been exciting, fulfilling, satisfying; if there had been no love there had been a strong degree of affection.

Now all had changed. Ryan came to Tracy because she was his wife, because he desired her body. Tracy would keep back her tears until he was asleep. She tried to tell herself that she gave in to him merely because she was his wife, and was doing her duty. And she knew that she lied to herself. She hungered for him, as much now as before. There were times when she thought she hated him, when she could cheerfully have thrown a shoe at his head in the hope of bringing to his face something other than the impersonal expression which had become habitual.

But the appalling thing was that through it all she still loved him. For the first time she learned for herself the truth of the maxim that love and hate could exist simultaneously. Whether they could do so happily was another matter.

Tracy was not happy. There had been no happiness for her since the moment Ryan had come upon her, stony-faced, on the beach. Some day she would leave him, his talk of being together forever notwithstanding. Living with him like this, in an atmosphere of impersonal politeness and unrelenting grimness, was sheer hell. Particularly because she loved him. In all likelihood she would always love him, she acknowledged despairingly to herself, but away from him she might be able to concentrate on other things, might be able to make a new life for herself.

She thought sometimes that it was only the idea that she would leave him that kept her sane. Not that she could do anything about it now. She would not leave Umhlowi while Allison needed her. Neither could she bear to hurt Ryan's grandmother, for Marie Demant had shown her so much kindness and affection.

But the time would come when she would have to think of herself first. By then, perhaps, her continued presence at Umhlowi would no longer mean so much to others, and they would understand.

Hopefully the time would come soon, for she had been feeling thoroughly out of sorts lately. Tired and without any appetite, nauseous when she woke in the morning, and often tearful. Emotion, she decided, could wreak havoc on body and spirit.

She was feeling particularly bad one morning while she was tending to Allison. Letitia had just brought in a tray bearing a fried egg with bacon and toast. It was almost seven weeks since the accident, and Allison was well on the way to recovery, but her right arm was still giving her trouble, so that there were things she could not yet do for herself. Tracy picked up knife and fork to cut the food for her. She looked down at the egg and the bacon, and suddenly the smell of it seemed to congeal in her nostrils. For a moment she felt so dizzy that she thought she would faint.

'Tracy!' Dimly she heard her sister's cry of concern, but she did not stop. Clasping a hand to her mouth she ran out of the room and to the bathroom.

Minutes later she came back into the room. She felt drained of all energy and was so pale that the freckles she had collected since coming to Umhlowi seemed to stand out on her cheeks, and Allison saw that she had splashed her face with water for her hairline was damp.

'Sorry about that,' Tracy said remorsefully.

'You're okay, sis?'

'Fine. I don't know what came over me.'

'Tracy . . .?' Allison was eyeing her, her eyes alive with concern and a touch of curiosity.

'Must be something I've eaten.'

'Think so?'

'Sure to be.' Tracy eyed the cooling food

doubtfully. 'I'm not sure I can cope with that though—even now.'

'No problem,' her sister said cheerfully. 'Derrick brought me some tea and a few biscuits before he went out. I'm not really hungry.'

Tracy drew a breath of relief. Moment by moment her strength was returning, but the sight of the food was off-putting. Keeping her eyes firmly away from the plate, she carried the tray back to the kitchen, and made her apologies to Letitia.

'You weren't feeling so hot yesterday either,' Allison observed when Tracy came back into the room.

'Must be some bug I've picked up.'

'Bug nothing.' Her sister laughed. 'I think you're pregnant.'

'Pregnant!' Tracy's head jerked up as she stared at Allison in horror. 'Oh no, I'm not pregnant,' she said too quickly.

'Are you sure?'

'Of course I am.' The words shot out emphatically. To be followed a few seconds later by uncertainty. 'At least . . .'

'Oh, Tracy.' Allison was laughing again. 'Think about it.'

Tracy stared a moment longer at her sister. Then she walked across to the window. A hand to an aching temple, she tried to think. Never one to write down dates, she did not have a diary to refer to. But memory could provide a frame of reference that was sometimes as efficient as a diary. And she did have memories.

She was imagining things, Allison's words had put an idea into her head, she told herself one minute. The next she admitted to herself that there could be some truth in the idea.

She turned from the window at last.

'Well?' Allison's eyes were on her, warm and concerned.

'I don't know. Maybe.'

'There's only one way to make sure.'

'Yes.'

'I hope it *is* a baby.' Allison's voice was suddenly fierce. 'I think I need to be an aunt.'

Because you may perhaps never be a mother? The words hung unspoken between them. Tracy crossed the room and gave her sister a hug.

'The best aunt any baby ever had,' she said, and saw that her sister's eyes were bright with unshed tears.

'You'll see a doctor?'

'This morning, if I can get an appointment.' She hesitated, knowing she had to speak, uncertain how the words would be received. At length, she said, 'If I *am* pregnant . . . don't say anything, Allie. Please?'

'To Derrick, do you mean?'

'To anybody. Not to Grandma and Patsy. Not . . . not to Ryan.'

'I promise.' There was sympathy in Allison's face. Tracy had never spoken of her marriage, but Allison was neither blind nor insensitive. 'You'll tell them all yourself when you're ready to.'

And when would that be? Tracy wondered later in the day, as she drove away from Umhlowi. If she was indeed pregnant, there would come a time when the shape of her body would make words unnecessary. Would she be ready to speak before then? The way things were with Ryan, could she bear to speak?

She did not go to the village, for she did not want anyone who knew her to see her coming out of a doctor's surgery. She drove instead a good thirty miles further, stopping at a place where she felt safe from gossip.

An hour later, armed with the facts—hadn't she known them already anyway?—she stopped the car at a lonely lagoon, and took the path down to the beach.

She went down to the wet sand nearest the water. In

the distance some children were playing with buckets and spades, piling up the sand into a castle, while their mothers sat nearby and chatted. Tracy walked the other way, in the direction of the lagoon.

A breeze was blowing and it lifted her hair behind her head and stung her face, and when a few tears escaped her eyes the breeze dried them, leaving small cold marks on her cheeks.

Seven-and-a-half months to the birth of the baby, the doctor had said. She was healthy and the pregnancy should be uncomplicated. Even the morning sickness would be temporary only. An elderly man, with a kind and weathered face, he had wished her happiness. She had thanked him, and had tried to smile.

A smile that had frozen on her face as she'd walked to the car.

Was it possible that she had not known until Allison had put the idea into her head? she wondered as she walked along the beach. She had put down her daily nausea to unhappiness when all the time she should have guessed it was morning sickness. It came to her now that perhaps she had known for some time. That perhaps she had used her unhappiness as an anchor to hold on to because she had been unwilling to face the truth.

Seven-and-a-half months to go. That would mean that the baby had been conceived almost immediately. On the day of the wedding perhaps, or in the days that had followed, before the accident. She hoped that was when it had happened, she thought suddenly, putting a protective hand over a stomach that was still flat. Poor baby, destined to be born to parents who did not want to be bound to each other. If it had been conceived at the very start of their marriage, at least it would have been created out of a passion that was more than just a physical thing, but that had stemmed from love on the part of the mother and very strong feelings of desire and affection on the part of the father. It would have been created in an atmosphere of joy. That must count for something, Tracy thought.

Her thoughts turned to the future. She had hoped to be able to leave Umhlowi as soon as circumstances permitted. Suddenly everything had changed. If there was a solution to her problem she did not know what it was.

A week later she had still said nothing to Ryan. All day she walked about with the knowledge that she had to tell him. She could think of nothing else. But something kept her from it. There was a part of her that dreaded his reaction. He might be pleased, on the other hand he might be angry, upset at the intruder that would link him to a woman he both distrusted and despised. Once Tracy would have been able to predict his reaction, but no longer. There was an additional reason why she wanted to keep the baby a secret. The polite but impersonal man she shared a roof and a bed with did not deserve her confidence.

She woke one morning to find that she was not alone in bed. Surprise accompanied the nausea that attacked her each day, for usually Ryan was up and out of the house before dawn.

'Good morning,' said a vibrant voice close to her ear.

'Did you oversleep?'

'On the contrary.' He sounded amused. It was a long time since she'd heard Ryan sound amused. 'I've been waiting for you to wake up.'

'Why?'

'Now there's a question to ask your husband.' He was lying so close to her that she could feel his breath warm on her cheek. A little pulse beat suddenly in her throat.

'Aren't you late for work?'

'I'm the boss, remember?' He had propped himself up on one elbow and was looking down at her as a finger went out to trace the shape of her lips.

'But . . .'

'But nothing,' he mocked her. 'Work can wait a while today. I have other plans.'

'Oh,' she responded inadequately.

'Is that all you can say?' He bent and let his tongue brush the slim column of her throat. 'Not that it matters, this isn't the time for conversation.'

It happened to be the time of day when she felt least well. 'Ryan . . .' she began.

He moved his head, closing her lips with his. After a moment he drew apart just far enough to whisper against her mouth, 'Do you know how sexy you look when you're asleep?'

A familiar path of fire started in her spine and began to travel downwards. 'I don't see myself when I'm asleep.'

'You don't, do you?' She heard laughter bubble in his throat. This was an unexpected return of the old Ryan. 'Let me tell you, you look incredibly sexy. That's why I decided not to get up.'

His arm went around her, his hand began to move lightly on her spine, the wisp of a nightgown that she wore was so thin that she felt every one of his fingers.

'You feel sexy too.' His voice had lost its amusement, had grown husky. 'Let's get this thing off.'

'Ryan . . .'

'We don't need barriers between us, I told you that once before.'

So easy to say when it was just a matter of clothes she thought painfully, as he drew the nightgown up and over her shoulders. The real barrier between them was intangible, and much harder to remove.

'Nice,' he said. 'Very nice.' And he drew her to him again.

It was Ryan's custom to sleep naked, and his chest was hard and rough against her breasts. She put her hand between their two bodies, letting it rest flat-palmed against him, loving the feel of his heart beneath her fingers. He began to kiss her again, and now she responded, her mouth opening willingly to his. It did not matter that he didn't love her. She knew only that she loved him, that she was carrying his baby. She didn't think beyond the day, not even beyond the moment. His mouth left hers and began to travel down her body, evoking an agonising response wherever it went. She began to kiss him too, his chest and his throat, shyly at first, because it was so long since he had relaxed his guard with her even when he was making love to her; and then, as her reserve melted, she began to kiss him with more ardour.

He turned her in his arms, wanting to lay her flat down on the bed. Perhaps the movement was too sudden, perhaps it was just that it would have happened anyway, but at that moment nausea struck her, violently, making her gasp.

He heard the sound and said, 'Tracy?'

'Ryan, I can't . . .'

She saw him frown. 'You're not backing out now?'

Her hand was in front of her mouth. 'I have to.'

'Is this what our marriage has become?' His voice was suddenly harsh. 'I'm your husband.'

'Ryan . . .' She had to get away from him, had to get to the bathroom.

'You were enjoying it! Damn you, Tracy, is there no end to the ways you frustrate me?'

She shook her head, she couldn't have answered him if she'd tried. Somehow she managed to push aside the heavy body that partly covered hers, and then she was running to the bathroom.

He must have followed her almost immediately, but she didn't know it until she felt his hand holding her forehead, supporting her head, helping her. She sank down at last on a small bathroom chair, feeling drained.

'Drink this.' He held out a glass of water. She tried to take it from him, but he continued to hold it while she sipped.

She took just a sip or two, and then she shook her head and he put the glass down.

'What's the matter, Tracy?'

She couldn't answer, even now it was an effort to speak.

'Are you ill?'

She shook her head.

'How do you know?' He was frowning.

'I know,' she whispered.

'Why do I get the feeling that this has happened before?' He paused a moment. 'It *has* happened, hasn't it?'

'Yes.'

He stood looking down at her, tall, virile, magnificent in his nakedness. He was still frowning. And then he said, 'Tracy—are you pregnant?'

In the week of feverish thought since she'd known about the baby she'd never imagined that Ryan would learn about it in this way.

'Well?' he demanded.

'Yes,' she admitted numbly. 'I'm pregnant.'

'How long have you known?'

There was no point in lying to him. 'About a week.'

'And you never said a word to me. It's my baby too, didn't you think I'd be interested?'

'I would have told you . . .'

'When?' His face was white, his mouth tight-lipped. 'The day you put on a maternity-dress?'

'Before then.'

There was an expression on his face that she had never seen before. She had seen him angry, had seen him openly contemptuous and arrogant. But this white-faced mask was something else. It was different from the way he'd looked on the beach when he'd surprised her with Derrick. Suddenly she was frightened.

'I suppose,' he said very deliberately, 'that it is my baby you're carrying?'

Weak as she was, anger flamed inside her, taking her to her feet. She struck him across the face, and had the satisfaction of seeing him pale even more.

'You were satisfied I was a virgin when I married you?' And when he nodded: 'I must have fallen pregnant almost right away. The baby is due in about seven months.' She sat down again. 'You can't think this is Derrick's baby?'

His eyes met hers. He was looking at her, still with an expression she couldn't explain, though it had changed somewhat in the last minute.

At length he said, 'No I don't think that. And I'm sorry I suggested it.'

Ryan was sorry? The words sounded strange in her ears.

'Get back to bed, Tracy.'

'I can't. Ryan, please.'

He gave a harsh laugh. 'Not with me. Just get to bed, and get some rest.'

'Yes,' she said weakly.

'I'm going to shower and shave now. On my way out of the house I'll stop by the kitchen and ask Letitia to bring you some tea.'

'Thank you, I'd appreciate that.' She said it as politely as if she was talking to a stranger who had just made her a friendly but rather meaningless offer. Nobody would have thought that just a little while ago passion had flamed between them.

'Tracy.' He stopped her as she walked out of the bathroom.

'Yes?'

'You don't need to worry. I won't bother you again.'

CHAPTER ELEVEN

I WON'T bother you again. The words were to repeat themselves in her mind over and over again in the days that followed. She had not given them any thought at the time they'd been said. There had just been the blessed relief of getting back into bed, of drinking the tea Letitia had brought her. She'd known there were questions that had to be resolved, with Ryan, also with herself. And she'd assumed that later, when Ryan came back to the house at the end of the day's work, they would talk.

But they did not talk. Not that day. Not in the days that followed. Worse still, Ryan began to go out at night. Night after night he came home late, sometimes at midnight, sometimes later. And when he came he would go to sleep on the narrow sofa that stood in the dressing-room. He never told Tracy where he went, and she was too proud to ask him.

One morning Tracy saw a red sports car draw up outside the house, and a svelte figure got out. Oh, no! Not Freda Antonis. Tracy had not even been able to face breakfast. How on earth was she going to cope with Freda?

'Ryan's not here,' she said politely as Freda installed herself on a verandah chair.

There sounded the husky laugh that jarred Tracy every time she had ever heard it. 'I didn't imagine he would be. I didn't come to see Ryan.'

Tracy looked at her suspiciously. 'You didn't?'

'Why, my dear, of course not. I speak to Ryan at other times than at ten on a week-day morning.'

A knot clenched tight in Tracy's stomach. It seemed that every time they met Freda baited her.

Very politely she said, 'Then why have you come?'

'To visit the invalid. I haven't met her yet.'

'Allison had a bad night. She's still sleeping.'

Now Freda would go. But she smiled and said, 'I'm sorry to hear it. But I came to see you as well.'

'I don't think we have much to say to each other.' Tracy's tone was flat.

The brilliant eyes sparkled with malice. 'I see marriage hasn't made you any surer of yourself.'

'I don't think you know me well enough to pass judgment.'

'Don't you? Tell me, are you enjoying the married state?'

'Yes.' Tracy shifted in her chair. 'Can I offer you some tea?'

'Tea's never been my drink, Ryan could tell you that, and I don't happen to be in the mood for anything stronger at this moment.' Freda leaned forward. She was like a spider, Tracy thought, relishing the idea of catching a victim in her web. 'So you are enjoying being a wife?'

Tracy looked her straight in the eye. 'Very much.'

'Even when your husband has fun without you?'

Tracy had already been sick once this morning, but now nausea attacked her again, seeming to grip every part of her body. 'You really are jealous of me aren't you?' she threw the words at Freda.

'Jealous? Good heavens, no. Nothing's changed between Ryan and myself. I thought you knew that.'

'I don't believe you.' Tracy kept her voice as controlled as she could.

'They do say there are none so blind as those who

won't see. What time did Ryan get home last night?' The husky laugh sounded once more when Tracy did not respond. 'Let me give you the answer in case you were asleep. After one.'

She was so close to the truth. So appallingly close. Tracy had lain awake, as she had done night after night, had heard the car draw up in the garage, and had looked at the clock before closing her eyes and pretending to be asleep when Ryan came into the room.

How could you do this to me, Ryan? she thought. Do you know that I feel torn apart inside, just as if you'd slashed at me with a knife?

She did not answer Freda's taunt. There was nothing she could say. She just let her nails bite into the palms of her hands and prayed that her composure would last until Freda chose to go.

But the other woman was not yet ready to give up her sport. A knowing smile curved her lips. 'I gather I'm not telling you something you didn't know. I wonder what you said to Ryan when he came in?'

'What passes between my husband and myself is our own business,' Tracy flashed.

'Maybe so. I do know it isn't sexy business.' And as Tracy stared at her, wondering how to counter this new attack: 'I happen to know the look of a man who's satisfied. Ryan isn't.'

Tracy drew a shaky breath. 'You're a vicious woman.'

'Vicious? Heavens no, just concerned. You're far too naive for a man like Ryan.'

'That may be your opinion,' Tracy said with an icy control. 'I don't care to discuss my private life with you.'

'If you say so.' Freda was not at all discomfited. She changed the subject. 'And how is your sister?'

'It will still be a while before she's herself again.'

'And you're not well either,' Freda observed.

'I'm fine, thank you.'

'You don't look fine at all.' The woman was looking at her assessingly. 'Thin and wan to say the least.'

Was this the prelude to another taunt? Defensively Tracy said, 'I'm really fine.'

'Well, it's only natural that you should feel out of sorts,' Freda went on. 'Ryan's neglect coupled with impending motherhood.'

Feeling stunned, Tracy met the amused eyes of the other woman. 'Motherhood?'

'Pregnancy. Babies,' Freda elaborated crisply.

'I don't want to talk about it!' The protest burst from Tracy's lips with unexpected vehemence.

'So you *are* pregnant.'

A strange look had appeared in Freda's face. It came to Tracy that she'd been trapped into revealing a fact that she'd imagined Freda had gleaned from Ryan. For a moment she wondered at the bitterness she saw in Freda's eyes.

Then Freda was laughing again. 'Marie Demant must be in her seventh heaven. A great grandchild, the one thing she always wanted.' She stood up. 'Clever Ryan, he has everything now. A baby and his fun into the bargain.'

Things did not improve in the months that followed. Ryan continued to go out almost every evening, and when he returned he would sleep in the dressing-room. Even when he was at home he kept his distance from Tracy. When they were together he was polite, even friendly, never cruel or arrogant as he'd been in the past. Yet sometimes Tracy wondered whether she didn't prefer the arrogance to what passed for friendliness now. She had hated Ryan when he was contemptuous, but at least she had been able to fight him then. How did one fight polite friendship?

As Freda had predicted, Marie Demant was delighted at the news of the baby. As were Tracy's mother and Allison and Patsy. Tiny sweaters and booties were being knitted. The birth was discussed constantly.

Discussion in which Tracy took little part. The baby was moving inside her, its kicking growing stronger every day. Tracy would put her hand over her stomach, and as she felt the movements against her palm she was swept with love for the child, but also with sadness. How could she join in any discussion when she herself did not know what the future would be? There was only one thing that she knew with certainty, and that was that life could not continue indefinitely the way it was now.

Fortunately, there were things that lifted her out of her preoccupation with the future. Allison was much better now, and her wedding to Derrick was a joyous occasion.

'He's a nice young man,' Lucille Galland said. 'And he really does love Allie, doesn't he?'

'Very much,' Tracy agreed, seeing the radiance in the couple's eyes when they looked at each other.

'I was wrong about him, Tracy.'

'So was I.'

'Well, all's well that ends well,' Lucille said happily.

Except that it wasn't going to end well at all. Not that this was the time to tell her mother about it. Allison's wedding was a time for happiness. Watching the pretty happy bride, Tracy knew it was a time for added happiness because Allison was walking again. As the doctor had predicted, she had a slight limp, but it was too early to tell whether it would be permanent. Either way it didn't seem to matter, because it obviously didn't mar her in Derrick's eyes.

'Isn't it strange,' Lucille observed, following Tracy's glance. 'I sent you all this way to put a stop to this wedding, and just look how things have worked out for you both.'

Stranger than her mother could know. She'd gone after Allison and had fallen in love. And then she'd gone after Allison again, and in just half an hour had destroyed everything she had held dear in the world.

'How are you feeling, darling?' Lucille asked.

'Just fine.'

'You look tired. But that's only natural.' Her mother's eyes went to Ryan, standing a little distance from them, talking to guests. 'I'm glad you have Ryan to care for you.'

Tracy was unable to answer. The most she could do was force a smile. Her mother looked so young today, young and happy and carefree. An older version of Allison. Life had not dealt kindly with Lucille Galland. Let her enjoy this day. Soon enough she would have to know the truth.

In the event it was Marie Demant who learned the truth first.

The baby was kicking vigorously at its mother's ribs, its birth no less than a month away, when Tracy went to have tea at Sea View. Patsy was out with friends, and Tracy and Marie were alone together.

It was a glorious day, and they drank their tea on the verandah that overlooked the sea. Marie had baked the melk-tert that Tracy loved, but the girl refused a second helping with a smile. 'They're gorgeous, Grandma, but I can't manage any more. I'm sure Patsy will be delighted to have the rest.'

'I've no doubt.' Marie laughed. 'That girl would sell her soul for melk-tert. In that she's like Ryan. I haven't seen my grandson for days, how is Ryan?'

Tracy's smile vanished. 'He's well. I'll have to tell him to visit you.'

'I suppose the fruit business is keeping him busy. What are his thoughts on the export market?'

Tracy did not know Ryan's thoughts on the export market, or on anything else for that matter. It was a long time since he had talked to her about anything meaningful.

She hesitated, then said, 'I don't know.'

'He must be excited about the baby?' Marie's eyes were on her face as she changed the subject.

It was hard to meet the steady gaze. Tracy shifted in her chair. 'He ... Yes, yes of course.'

'Good.' Tracy heard rather than saw Mrs Demant put down her cup and stand up. 'Wait here a moment, will you?'

Tracy pushed her chair away from the table and looked across the sea. A yacht was skimming the waves. There was something so unfettered, so carefree in the sight.

The baby moved inside her, and she put her hand on her stomach. Poor baby, she said silently. My poor baby.

Absorbed in her thoughts, she did not hear Marie's footsteps. Only when a voice said, 'This is for you, Tracy dear,' did she turn.

Ryan's grandmother was holding out what looked like a jewellery-box. Something in her face made Tracy suddenly hesitant.

'Tracy,' Mrs Demant prompted.

She had to take the box then. 'Open it,' she heard the soft command, and with fingers that were trembling she did so.

'It's beautiful!' The exclamation escaped her at the sight of the necklace that lay on the purple velvet. It was made of pearls and sapphires, and it was the most elegant thing Tracy had ever seen.

'Like it?'

'It ... It's incredible.'

'Will you put it on? I want to see how you look.'

Tracy took the necklace from its velvet bed. She was

lifting it to her throat when reality struck. The colour drained from her face as she looked at Mrs Demant.

'I can't. I'm sorry.'

'But it's yours, my dear.'

'No . . .' The word came out on a stifled sob.

Marie ignored her emotion. 'A Demant heirloom. Have you any idea, Tracy, how happy you're making me? How I've longed for great grandchildren.'

Just as Freda had predicted. Tracy swallowed, her throat was dry and painful.

'I had intended giving you the necklace when the baby was born,' Marie said.

'Then why are you giving it to me now?'

'It seems the right moment.'

Tracy looked up and met the eyes that were on her face. Dark eyes, steady and perceptive, so much like Ryan's.

She knows! The thought hit her suddenly. Grandma knows.

'I can't take this.' Fingers that were cold as ice put the necklace back in its box.

'Why, Tracy, why?'

'Because I'm leaving Ryan.' Somehow Tracy got the words out, and then she put her hands over her face to hide the tears that she could no longer hold back.

It was a while before she could talk again, and Marie Demant seemed to understand, for she did not press her.

Later, when the tears had dried, Ryan's grandmother said matter-of-factly, 'I think it's time we talked.'

'You don't seem surprised.'

'I'm not.' There was a wry smile at Tracy's startled look. 'I may be old, dear, but I'm not blind. I know when something's wrong.'

'Then you know everything?'

'None of the details. Oh, Tracy, you haven't fooled

me, and neither has Ryan. For months now I've held my tongue, God alone knows how. But the time has come for me to know why two people who obviously love each other are looking quite so unhappy.'

'Ryan doesn't love me.'

'Rubbish,' dismissed his grandmother crisply.

'He never did. He . . .' She shot a look at Marie and decided that she was a thoroughly modern woman who would not mind the word. 'He desired me.'

'Go on.'

The story came out. How she'd been determined to reveal to Allison that Derrick was nothing but a playboy. How Ryan had come upon them on the beach.

'*Would* you have seduced Derrick?' Quite incredibly Marie's eyes were sparkling with laughter.

'Of course not! It was all supposed to be a matter of timing.'

'When you're as old as I am you'll know that timing seldom works.' The laughter faded. 'Didn't you explain to Ryan?'

'I tried. He was furious. He didn't want to listen.'

'You could have tried again.'

'Not when I saw how he felt about me. I came to realise that if he couldn't trust me then our marriage was . . . was not worth anything.'

'And now you're going to leave him.' Marie was amazingly calm.

'After the baby is born.'

'I see.'

'No you don't!' Tracy's head jerked up urgently. 'I'm going to leave the baby at Umhlowi.'

It had taken a lot to break Marie Demant's composure. But it was broken now.

'You'd do that?'

'Not because I don't care! It'll probably tear my heart out!'

'Then why?' It was asked very gently.

'I can't give you an easy answer, Grandma. But I've done a lot of thinking. In fact I've done nothing but think these last months. The baby means so much to you. To Ryan too—I happen to know that he wants a child.'

'Don't you want one?'

'Of course I do! So very much.' Tracy dashed fresh tears from her eyes. 'But the baby will be a Demant. At Umhlowi with Ryan, with Allison, with you and Patsy, it will have the life I can never provide for it on my own. Allie may never have children, she'll love this baby so much, she'll take care of it as if it was her own.'

'What about you, Tracy? Where do you fit into all this?'

Tracy's throat was so raw now that it felt sandpapered. 'I won't be going back to Durban. I'll try to find a job in Margate. I'll use my legacy to buy a car, and if Ryan will let me, I'll visit Umhlowi as often as I can. And Allie will bring the baby to see me.'

'So you have everything worked out.'

'I've tried. It hasn't been easy.' Tracy shifted on the chair as the baby kicked inside her. 'You may as well know, I'm desperately unhappy about it. But it seems the only way.'

She turned her face towards the ocean again. Fresh tears choked her throat and blinded her eyes. Her heart was breaking. If only Marie did not try to argue with her.

But Ryan's grandmother didn't question her further. She took back the necklace, and began to talk quietly of other things, seeming to expect no response from Tracy, who had reached the stage where she could not have spoken if she had tried.

Lucy Marie Demant was born on a night when a

tropical storm rent the sky and slashed the oceans. Tracy loved her the moment she saw her. Except that love seemed an inadequate word to describe what she felt. The well of maternal feeling that flowed from her into this tiny perfect being was not the gentle emotion she had envisaged. It was something fierce and primeval, overwhelming and all-encompassing.

Her love for Ryan was the love of a woman for a man. It was made up of many things. Sexual desire, a wanting to be with him in joy and sorrow. A craving to share her life with him—notwithstanding the fact that she knew it would never happen.

Her love for her daughter was a very different thing. It shook Tracy, penetrated to the very core of her being. She had never known motherhood could be like this.

Ryan was a proud father. Tracy saw the expression in his eyes when he looked down at the baby asleep in her crib; when he held her, a little awkwardly, in his big hands. There was love in his eyes as well as pride. It was an expression that brought a lump to Tracy's throat. By rights they should be able to love their child together, a mother and a father watching their daughter grow up. But that could never be.

One night, a month after Lucy was born, Tracy wakened to the cry of a hungry baby in the next room. She left her bed, walked softly past the door of the dressing-room where Ryan lay sleeping, and lifted Lucy from her crib. As she put the baby to her breast and listened to the tiny purring sounds that accompanied the sucking, she was overwhelmed anew with her feelings of maternal love. There were no bounds to the things she would do for this tiny being that she had carried inside her for nine months. She would work for her, she would even kill for her, if necessary. There was nothing she would not do for her.

Well, almost nothing. Could she leave Lucy here, with her father and her Aunt Allison? To grow up at Umhlowi, surrounded by every luxury a child could have?

No! She knew all at once, and quite definitely, that it was the one thing she could not do. Staring down at the infant, her eyes suddenly clouding with tears, Tracy realised that the revelation which had just come to her was not new. It had been in her mind since the moment that Lucy had uttered her first cry. But until this moment she had not been ready to admit it to herself.

Footsteps sounded behind her. She had not heard Ryan coming from the dressing-room. She turned to look at him, her pulses quickening at sight of the tall figure, nude to the waist. Then she became aware of her bare breast, of the tears in her eyes, and she bent her head to the baby.

A big hand gently touched the baby's cheek, then rested, just as gently, on Tracy's breast. Tracy shuddered.

'Very lovely,' she heard him say.

She did not answer.

After a moment, he said, 'You're crying?'

She shook her head.

The hand left her breast, and cupped her chin, so that she had to look at him. 'You *are* crying. Tracy, why?'

Her throat was dry, but she had to speak. She should have spoken long ago.

'I can't leave Lucy,' she got out.

'Well of course you can't.'

'You don't understand.' Her throat ached. 'I'm taking Lucy away.'

'You're not taking Lucy anywhere.' Ryan's tone was firm.

'Freda said you'd . . .' She stopped. No good telling

him that Freda had intimated from the start that all he wanted from Tracy was a child. That he would do everything he could to keep the baby. Fiercely now, she said, 'I love this baby, Ryan.'

'So do I.'

'I can't leave here without her.'

'Neither of you will be leaving.'

She stared at him.

'Umhlowi is your home,' Ryan said. 'Your home and Lucy's. *Our* home. Surely you know that, my darling?'

He was still holding her chin, and now a thumb began a slow stroking movement along her throat. It was so long since he had caressed her, since he had made any attempt to make love to her. She tried to quell the response that was starting inside her, tried to tell herself that he was playing games with her, that he was looking for ways to keep Lucy for himself. But the long hard body was so close to her that her senses were suddenly on fire, and she knew only that she loved him, and that the months alone in the big double bed had been an ordeal.

'Surely you know it?' he asked again.

She shook her head, unable to talk.

She heard him make a little noise in his throat, and then the hand that had been holding her chin dropped from her as he walked away.

Lucy was still suckling, and Tracy bent to kiss the soft head. Not for the first time she had angered Ryan and been rejected by him. If only she could hold back the tears. This was a moment for strength and assertiveness; she could not let emotion get the better of her. But the tears fell unchecked.

She jerked at the touch of ice at her throat.

'Keep still,' Ryan ordered, and she felt him tighten a clasp at the back of her neck.

'What are you doing?' she asked alarmed.

'Look.' He was holding a hand-mirror so that she could see in to it. Around her neck was a gold chain with a lovely diamond pendant that nestled in the hollow between her breasts.

Tracy caught her breath. 'No!'

'You'll get a bracelet to match it when we have our second child,' Ryan said, as if he had not heard the protest.

'Ryan . . .'

'And the ear-rings on one of our wedding anniversaries.'

'There won't be any more children. Any anniversaries.' Somehow she got the words out.

She felt him stiffen. Then he said, 'Hasn't Lucy finished feeding yet?'

The baby had stopped sucking some minutes ago, but Tracy had continued to hold her against her breasts.

'Put her down,' Ryan said.

She didn't have to take his orders. But it was indeed time to let the baby sleep. With shaking hands Tracy changed a wet nappy, then put the baby lovingly back in her crib.

As she turned back to Ryan, who had been watching her all the while, she lifted her fingers to the necklace. 'I can't take this,' she said.

His hands moved to her throat, covering her fingers, preventing her from undoing the clasp. 'You refused Grandma's gift. You won't refuse mine.'

The hands on hers were warm and vibrant. For a moment she let her fingers rest beneath his, unable to withdraw them, feeling as if they were tied to his by an unbreakable cord. Then, summoning some effort of will, she moved away from him.

'You know about that?' She wished that she could keep her voice from shaking.

'I know. I know many things about you, Tracy.'

His voice was so soft, so caressing. It set up a violent reaction inside her. There was a kind of happiness, and hope too, but these were emotions she suppressed almost immediately. After months of coldness Ryan was showing warmth and tenderness again. What was he up to? She knew that she could not let him hurt her again.

'There won't be any more children. Any anniversaries,' she repeated. 'I'm leaving you.'

'I won't let you.' His voice was husky.

'You mean you want to continue with this marriage?'

'Yes.'

Perhaps he felt that little Lucy needed a father as well as a mother, and that she should spend her first years at Umhlowi. That was all it could be. Concern for his daughter.

'For how long?' she asked dully.

'Forever. Isn't that what we promised each other, Tracy darling?'

A promise she had made in joy and love. A promise she yearned to keep, even now. Despite the fact that it wasn't possible.

'There's no point in going on with this charade,' she protested. Her voice was very low, it was the only way she could keep from crying again.

Ryan touched her cheek. Very gently he brushed a strand of tousled hair from her forehead. 'It won't be a charade.'

'What will it be?' Anger gave her voice sudden strength. 'I can't stand another day of this empty existence. Pretending to be cheerful when inside I feel as if I'm being torn to shreds.'

'Tracy . . .'

She was too overwrought to let him speak. 'You talk of promises. How do you think I've felt all these months, Ryan? Lying awake night after night waiting for you to come home? Alone in a bed that was meant for both of us?'

'Do you think it was easy for me?' he demanded roughly.

'You had Freda,' she threw at him recklessly.

The tall figure grew tense. The hand on her hair dropped as he took a step away from her.

'That's the second time you've mentioned Freda tonight. Why?'

'You know why,' she stormed. 'You've been with Freda all this time!'

His eyes were cold. 'You've been jumping to conclusions.'

'I didn't have to do any jumping. Freda was only too willing to tell me. At least she was honest.'

'What exactly did Freda tell you?' Ryan asked coldly.

'That you were lovers. That she couldn't marry you because her ex-husband made it impossible. That you never intended breaking off your relationship with her after we were married.'

'Anything else?'

'That you only married me because you wanted a child. Because your grandmother wanted a great grandchild.'

'I see,' he said after a long moment. 'That explains why you told Grandma that . . .' He broke off.

His voice hardened as he spoke again. 'You believed Freda.'

Tracy was taken aback. 'Not at first. Not that first time, before we were married. But then . . . What was I to think, Ryan? You showed no interest in me. You stayed out late every night.'

'You believed I was with Freda.'

'She knew what time you came home.'

'Because,' he said deliberately, 'she happened to see me in the lounge of the village hotel. We talked,

Tracy, but there were other people with us every time. And we never arranged to meet.'

There was hardness in Ryan's tone, but there was also conviction. Tracy believed him.

'Why did Freda say the things she did?' she wanted to know.

'Perhaps Patsy was right when she said Freda was jealous.' Ryan was thoughtful. 'Jealousy can be dangerous. Freda and I ... There was something once, Tracy, I've told you before I was no saint, but it didn't last long. There was never any question of marriage despite what she told you. And it was over by the time you came on the scene.'

The relationship with Freda might have been over for Ryan, but perhaps the woman had gone on hoping that he would come back to her. Tracy felt a moment of sympathy with her, for she knew quite how potent Ryan's appeal could be.

She looked at her husband, tall and tanned and devastatingly sexy. His hair was ruffled, and his bare chest was broad and inviting. She wanted nothing so much as to be held against it. 'Why *did* you stay out late every night?' she asked.

'Because if I'd been at home I'd have wanted to make love to you.' He took her in his arms. 'Do you know how hard it's been to stay away from you?'

She leaned her head against him, glorying in the hardness of his chest, in the beating of his heart against her cheek, in the familiar scent of him in her nostrils. For the first time she allowed herself some hope.

'You didn't have to stay away,' she said.

'You were pregnant. And I'd treated you so badly.'

His voice was uncertain. Ryan uncertain? It made him strangely vulnerable, made her love him even more.

'I felt I had to wait till after the baby was born to come back to your bed,' he said. 'Was I wrong?'

'You were. Oh yes, you were.' She thought of the many lonely months. The unhappiness. 'If only I'd known.'

Ryan's arms had folded around her, his hands were exploring her back, sliding beneath the silk nightgown to caress her shoulders. 'You should have trusted me,' he said.

Tracy leaned back to look at him. 'You didn't trust me either.'

'I know. You tried to explain, and I didn't let you.' Ryan was silent a moment. 'Oh, I admit I was beside myself when I found you on the beach with Derrick. I thought . . .'

Drawing her back to him, he went on more gently. 'But I got over my mistrust months ago. When you refused my grandmother's gift it was merely confirmation of what I already knew. There's not a single calculating bone in you, my darling.'

Was it possible to be quite so happy? Such intense happiness after so much despair—it was almost too much to take in. Tracy wanted only to be close to Ryan, to stay in her arms, to feel his lips on hers. But there were still things to be said before she could give herself over to such luxury.

'You thought I'd tricked you into asking me to marry you.'

'For a while,' he admitted.

'I did try to trap Derrick,' Tracy confessed.

'For what you thought was a good reason. You were trying to protect Allison.'

'But at the time you thought . . . Why wouldn't you let me go?'

The hands that had been on her back went to her head now, cupping it on either side, drawing it back, so that Ryan could look into her eyes.

'Because I loved you. That's why I was so angry, my darling. The women I'd known were mostly after what I could give them. Freda. Others before her. And then I met you, and I fell crazily in love. And I couldn't bear to think I'd been wrong about you.'

He'd fallen in love with her! The words she'd longed to hear for so long. Her pulses were suddenly pounding.

'Do you understand?' Ryan asked.

Understand? 'You said you'd fallen in love with me,' she said urgently.

'You sound so surprised.'

'You never told me.'

Ryan made a sound in his throat. 'My God, Tracy, what do you think all we've been through has been about? Even at the worst of it, when I thought you were after Derrick, I loved you so much that I knew I couldn't let you go.'

She looked up at him, her eyes shining like emeralds in the soft glow of the night-light. 'You never said anything.'

'My darling girl, I thought it was obvious. You know I connived to keep you at Umhlowi. I fell in love with you almost the moment I saw you. When you rescued the kitten from the tree. Tracy darling.' His voice roughened. 'I've missed you so much. And I want you so badly. Do we still have to wait?'

'No.' She slid her hands between them, letting them lie flat-palmed against his chest. 'We don't have to wait.'

'We have so much loving to make up.' There was a break in his voice.

She slanted him a provocative smile. 'Let's start right now.'

'My lovely seductress.' He lifted her to him, and began to kiss her, his lips never breaking contact with hers as he carried her to their bed.

Coming Next Month In Harlequin Presents!

839 BITTER ENCORE—Helen Bianchin
Nothing can erase the memory of their shared passion. But can an estranged couple reunite when his star status still leaves no room for her in his life—except in his bed?

840 FANTASY—Emma Darcy
On a secluded beach near Sydney, a model, disillusioned by her fiancé, finds love in the arms of a stranger. Or is it all a dream—this man, this fantasy?

841 RENT-A-BRIDE LTD—Emma Goldrick
Fearful of being forced to marry her aunt's stepson, an heiress confides in a fellow passenger on her flight from Denver—never thinking he'd pass himself off as her new husband!

842 WHO'S BEEN SLEEPING IN MY BED?—Charlotte Lamb
The good-looking playwright trying to win her affection at the family villa in France asks too many questions about her father's affairs. She's sure he's using her.

843 STOLEN SUMMER—Anne Mather
She's five years older, a friend of the family's. And he's engaged! How can she take seriously a young man's amorous advances? Then again, how can she not?

844 LIGHTNING STORM—Anne McAllister
A young widow returns to California and re-encounters the man who rejected her years before—a man after a good time with no commitments. Does lightning really strike twice?

845 IMPASSE—Margaret Pargeter
Unable to live as his mistress, a woman left the man she loves. Now he desires her more than ever—enough, at least, to ruin her engagement to another man!

846 FRANGIPANI—Anne Weale
Her sister's offer to find her a millionaire before they dock in Fiji is distressing. She isn't interested. But the captain of the ship finds that hard to believe....

Readers rave about Harlequin American Romance!

" ...the best series of modern romances
I have read...great, exciting, stupendous,
wonderful."
—S.E.*, Coweta, Oklahoma

" ...they are absolutely fantastic...going to be
a smash hit and hard to keep on the
bookshelves."
—P.D., Easton, Pennsylvania

"The American line is great. I've enjoyed
every one I've read so far."
—W.M.K., Lansing, Illinois

" ...the best stories I have read in a long
time."
—R.H., Northport, New York

*Names available on request.

You're invited to accept 4 books and a surprise gift Free!

Acceptance Card

Mail to: Harlequin Reader Service®

In the U.S.
2504 West Southern Ave.
Tempe, AZ 85282

In Canada
P.O. Box 2800, Postal Station A
5170 Yonge Street
Willowdale, Ontario M2N 6J3

YES! Please send me 4 free Harlequin American Romance® novels and my free surprise gift. Then send me 4 brand new novels as they come off the presses. Bill me at the low price of $2.25 each —an 11% saving off the retail price. There are no shipping, handling or other hidden costs. There is no minimum number of books I must purchase. I can always return a shipment and cancel at any time. Even if I never buy another book from Harlequin, the 4 free novels and the surprise gift are mine to keep forever.

154 BPA-BPGE

_____
Name   (PLEASE PRINT)

_____
Address   Apt. No.

_____
City   State/Prov.   Zip/Postal Code

This offer is limited to one order per household and not valid to present subscribers. Price is subject to change.   ACAR-SUB-1

Take 4 books
& a surprise gift
FREE

SPECIAL LIMITED-TIME OFFER

Mail to   **Harlequin Reader Service®**

In the U.S.   In Canada
2504 West Southern Ave.   P.O. Box 2800, Station "A"
Tempe, AZ 85282   5170 Yonge Street
                       Willowdale, Ontario M2N 6J3

YES! Please send me 4 free Harlequin Presents® novels and my free surprise gift. Then send me 8 brand-new novels every month as they come off the presses. Bill me at the low price of $1.75 each ($1.95 in Canada)—a 11% saving off the retail price. There are no shipping, handling or other hidden costs. There is no minimum number of books I must purchase. I can always return a shipment and cancel at any time. Even if I never buy another book from Harlequin, the 4 free novels and the surprise gift are mine to keep forever.

Name   (PLEASE PRINT)

Address   Apt. No.

City   State/Prov.   Zip/Postal Code

This offer is limited to one order per household and not valid to present subscribers. Price is subject to change.   DOP–SUB–1